Of Face Value

Carol Harper

PublishAmerica
Baltimore

First printing

Of Face Value is based on the true story of Carol Harper. Names and
identities of some of the people and places in this book have been
changed to protect their privacy. A few of the characters and events
have been combined for purposes of dramatization. Several dates
have been changed in order to condense the story.

ISBN: 1-4137-9805-5 (softcover)
ISBN: 978-1-4489-9908-8 (hardcover)
PUBLISHED BY PUBLISHAMERICA, LLLP
www.publishamerica.com
Baltimore

Printed in the United States of America

This book is dedicated to
Deborah Underwood Leslie,
the nurse who saved my life.

Acknowledgments

I want to thank my daughter, Christa Minter, who helped me write, organize and type the manuscript.

With love and gratitude for my sisters and brothers: Marilyn Cole, Chuck Mooshian, Jim Mooshian, Donna Stites, Deborah Wallace, Rick Mooshian and Robert Mooshian. I appreciate all of your encouragement and support during the writing of this book. To my mom, Grace Mooshian, who gave me love and encouragement.

Thanks to Wil Denmark for helping me outline the story and selecting the title.

Dara Marks for introducing me to the transformational arc and her critique of the story.

Dr. Ted Baehr for his expertise on the story and his encouragement throughout the writing process.

Careful readers who gave their comments and suggestions: Maureen Fleming Clark, Sylvia Wygoda, Kimberly Christopher, Diana and Matt Stroup, Bob von Allmen, Mary Long, Deborah Thorman, Dr. Olga Fairfax, Gary Cheatham, Sandy

Taffle, Dr. Abe Cardwell, Jim Penney, Jill Winkler, Carol Morrison, Libby Wilkins, Dr. Steve Nudelman, Andrea Rock, Janice Hayes, Lisa Rice, J.Tore Knos, Jan DeRossett, Pat Warren and Jennifer Jones.

A special thanks to Linda Gibson for helping me with my computer and her support.

Thanks to PublishAmerica for believing in me. In great appreciation for my editor and artist for designing the book cover.

I appreciate you all for making my dream a reality.

Prologue

July 7, 1974

The trauma team was ready for the young female victim as the ambulance backed up to the emergency entrance at Northridge Hospital. They immediately wheeled her critically injured body into the emergency room where Dr. George Clayton, a young doctor in his late-twenties, began calling out directives. The woman's body was transferred from the gurney onto the exam table and several sensing devices were immediately hooked up to her body. The trauma team went to work assessing her injuries.

"Damn it! We're about to lose her," Dr. Clayton warned at one point. "Paddles now!"

A trauma nurse prepared the electrical paddles and handed them off to Dr. Clayton. He positioned them on the dying woman and yelled, "Clear!" before sending the electric current through her body. The oscilloscope continued to show a straight line.

"Again. Clear!" He zapped her again. Still no change. It wasn't until he sent the current through her body a third time that the oscilloscope measured a faint heartbeat. The trauma team resumed their work.

The young woman was far from being out of danger, but at least she was momentarily stabilized. Her face, bluish-black in color, was swollen to twice its normal size and looked anything but human. Gone were all the physical features that made this woman who she was. She was unrecognizable—her beautiful face was gone...

Chapter One

One year earlier...

As the Inaugural Ball was just about to begin, Lisa Davenport paused in front of the oversized mirror situated in the hallway of the lavish hotel and adjusted her long, red velvet dress. Attending the ball was just one of the many perks of her job as public relations assistant at the Sheraton Park Hotel in Washington, D.C. Tonight she would mingle, oversee the hotel photographer, and make sure everyone was having a good time. Confident in her appearance, she took a deep breath and turned from the mirror to join the others downstairs who were waiting for a glimpse of the new President of the United States.

Before descending the steps to the main lobby, she leaned over the balcony's brass banister to survey the crowd. From her vantage point, she could see the ballroom was filled with Washington's elite. The women were exquisitely dressed in flowing, colorful gowns offset by mink and rabbit stoles. They wore their hair in topknots so that their gleaming diamond earrings would not be hidden from view.

The men were handsomely dressed in their best tuxedos with starched white shirts and bow ties. One thing was for certain: everyone in attendance was wealthy—and didn't hesitate to show it. The ballroom exuded an aura of power and prestige.

In the direction of the red carpet, reporters and photographers lined the aisle and flashes of light continually ricocheted off the walls as the photographers snapped picture after picture. This was definitely the place to be this evening.

Feeling as though she should pinch herself to make sure this wasn't a dream, she descended the stairs. Nearing the landing, she missed the low murmurings and whispers of the people around her. Her mind was on meeting the President and she was unaware people were admiring her. No matter where she went, or what she was wearing, she had the ability to turn heads even from an early age. Many times she was oblivious to the fact that she was so pretty even though men had always complimented her. She thought men told *all* women they were beautiful to get what they wanted.

She spied head of security Jim Stafford and made her way to security barricades to speak with him. Jim, a long time employee of the hotel, always kept her informed as to when political figures and movie stars were scheduled to stay at the hotel.

"Good evening, Lisa," he greeted and smiled.

"Good evening, Mr. Stafford. You look handsome this evening," she complimented in her charming southern drawl. She was born and raised in Little Rock, Arkansas and never lost her accent.

His eyes roamed over her from head to toe. In his opinion, she was the essence of beauty and he wasn't afraid to admit he had a crush on her. Who didn't? The young public relations assistant had it all. She was beautiful, charming, had a terrific figure, and a vivacious personality to top it all off.

"You always look great, Lisa. But tonight," he sighed heavily and put his hand over his heart, "you take my breath away."

No stranger to compliments, she reflexively flashed her proud smile. She knew that her looks played an important role in her successes over the years but wanted to believe that her intelligence also played an equally significant role. "Thank you, Mr. Stafford."

"I heard a rumor you might be leaving us. Are you planning to move to Atlanta?"

News travels fast, she thought. "It looks that way. My fiancé Brian just got a promotion that will take him to Atlanta. It's either move with him or call off the wedding."

"That's too bad," he replied, still unable to take his eyes of her. "You know, if you two would happen to call it off, you can always give me a call."

Outwardly, she smiled at his proposal. Inwardly, she was flattered but knew it would never work. It was her firm policy never to date men at work. She bid him a good night and walked away, while his eyes were on the revealing slit that went up the back of her dress.

"Hey! Where do you think you're going, mister?" Jim commanded a response from the tall, lanky, awkward-looking man who'd managed to slip by him while he'd been watching Lisa walk away.

"It's me, Peter Black," the man answered indicating the camera hanging around his neck and flashing his pass.

"Peter, I didn't recognize you all dressed up in your tux with your hair slicked back. Go right ahead," Jim directed, somewhat embarrassed that he didn't recognize the hotel photographer.

Lisa overheard the exchange and laughed inwardly. She had to admit that even she almost didn't recognize Peter this evening. His usual straggly, long, dark hair was slicked back, and his normally rugged, razor-stubbled face was freshly shaven. He even wore a designer suit!

Peter was yet another one of her admirers. She considered him a dear friend, and she cared for him. He'd shared his feelings for her often, which always made her feel uncomfortable. He'd been trying for almost a year to win her over, but she would never date someone she worked with so closely. Her career was of utmost importance to her and she didn't want anything or anyone to jeopardize it.

Her thoughts returned to the task at hand. "Peter, I was thinking, we should get a few pictures of the senators and congressmen, before the President arrives." Not waiting for a response, she added, "You *have* to get a picture of me with the President."

"Security's too tight. We'll never get close enough for a good picture."

"Yes, we will," she said in a matter-of-fact tone. She was a determined individual and usually got what she wanted.

Peter shook his head and rolled his eyes. "Whatever you say, Lisa," he humored her. "Hey there's the senator from New York. Let's get his picture. What's his name again?"

"Senator Rueben." She double-checked the pins in her hair, worrying that one might come loose. This was a special night and she wanted to look perfect.

The two navigated their way through the crowd to reach the tall, broad-shouldered handsome senator who exuded confidence. Although he was in deep discussion with the new speaker of the house, she politely interrupted their conversation and introduced herself.

"Senator, would you mind posing for a picture?" she asked after the introductions had been made. She exuded a certain charisma about her that no one could refuse.

"Not at all," he replied, somewhat surprised by her boldness. He was drawn to her like a magnet.

Peter focused his camera and directed, "Lisa, move closer to the senator." She did so and he snapped away.

When she was satisfied he'd taken enough to ensure that at least one would turn out, she stepped away and directed him to take some shots of the senator and the speaker of the house.

Yes, she had the perfect job.

Her mood changed when her thoughts turned to Brian Caulder, her fiancé. He was handsome, successful, and confident—all the qualities she was looking for in a man…and, they looked good together. Everyone said they made the perfect couple. She loved him and wanted to marry him. But move to Atlanta?

Peter stirred her from her musings. "Lisa, you've probably already heard this a million times tonight, but you look beautiful."

Yes, she had, but it made her feel good about herself to hear it again. She looked at him and he was staring so intently at her, making her feel uncomfortable. She could tell he was about to express his feelings to her, again, even though she'd made it perfectly clear to him that she enjoyed his friendship, but nothing more. She wasn't attracted to him. Yes, he was funny and made her laugh; yes, he cared for her and showed genuine concern for her life, but he wasn't for her. And he spent way too much time talking about feelings and trying to reach her soul. Her soul was just fine.

"Look, Lisa, I know we've been friends for a while but I'd really like to take you out sometime. Please don't move to Atlanta. You'll never find another job like this one; you know that better than anyone. Your friends are here, not in Atlanta." He paused and his voice softened when he added, "I'm here."

Lisa sighed. "Peter, that's really nice of you but—"

"I know you're engaged to Brian," he continued, "but Lisa, I'm in love with you. There, I said it, and I'm sorry to spring this on you like this, but I couldn't hide my true feelings any longer. Come on Lisa, let's give us a try."

She looked into his pleading eyes. He'd often told her that he loved her spirit, her soul, and her caring and compassionate nature but that didn't make a difference. She didn't feel the same way about him as he did for her.

"Peter, I'll be honest with you." She tried to be careful with her words because she didn't want to hurt his feelings. "You have several endearing qualities that I admire. You're smart, considerate, caring, and generous, and I'm flattered that you feel the way you do. But I'm going to marry Brian. We're perfect for each other." To herself she added, you're just not my type, Peter. "Look, let's talk about this later; we need to get back to work."

Lisa spied Congressman Brogan from Illinois, the media's favorite, loading up his plate at the buffet table. She was just about to tap on his shoulder for a picture when she heard her name being called by Washington socialite Pearle Mesta. Pearle had invited Lisa to several of her exclusive formal parties in the past. The thought that she was included among such guests as ambassadors, congressmen, and senators made her feel important. Would she lose it all when she married Brian?

"Ms. Davenport," the graceful older lady called. "I'm looking for Ms. Dubois. Have you seen her?"

"No, I haven't. But she's around here somewhere." Lisa stood on her tip toes and scanned the crowd for Christine Dubois, her boss. She, too, needed to find her to check in.

As the hotel's public relations director, Christine could be a bit bossy at times, but for the most part, she and Lisa worked well together. Christine depended on her to keep things running smoothly and her boss would have a hard time replacing her if she left. She needed to make a decision so she could tell Ms. Dubois.

Scanning the room, she finally found the director sipping on a martini near the bar. She was about to head in that direction when Peter jabbed her in the side.

"Lisa, quick!" he said, pointing to the side entrance. "The President's about to arrive."

Lisa took a moment to straighten her gown before allowing Peter to usher her through the crowd. They needed to be much closer to the entrance in order to get a good picture. They joined the others who were pushing and shoving to get closer. Security was tight and the two were stopped just short of the procession by a silver makeshift barricade.

Secret Service men were everywhere and seemed to outnumber the members of the press. Security was tight and everyone in the room that night had an extensive FBI background check performed, even Lisa and Peter.

When the two reached the female security officer, they showed their passes. She wasn't impressed.

"These passes don't allow you to pass through here." The officer scowled.

Lisa hadn't spent the past few hours meticulously perfecting her appearance for a memorable evening with the President only to be turned away by an arrogant, power-seeking security officer.

"Hey, Lisa," a deep voice whispered from behind.

Turning, she came face-to-face with George, a top-level Secret Service agent she had dated briefly. He brought his finger to his lips, beckoning her silence, then unhooked a rope from the cordoned off area and motioned for her and Peter to go through. Her path to the President was now unobstructed.

Cynthia Norris, a reporter with Channel 27 News, didn't miss the gesture and called out. "Why does she get to go through?" The tone of her voice clearly conveyed her displeasure.

George, somewhat embarrassed that he'd been caught bending the rules, replied, "She's with the hotel."

Lisa and Peter made their way to where the President would enter the ballroom just as *Hail to the Chief* began to play. Within seconds, the President, accompanied by his wife and two daughters, entered the room and waved to the cheering crowd. He occasionally stopped to shake hands and pose for a picture. The flickering of camera flashes filled the room.

Lisa's heart rate increased as the President neared the area she and Peter were standing. When he was right in front of them, she reached out to shake his hand and just as he took her hand in his firm grip, Peter snapped a shot. Perfect!

She was still reeling from having shaken the President's hand when Peter commented, "That's going to be a great picture, Lisa." He fidgeted with his camera for a moment before adding, "I'm going to take a quick break to get another lens for the camera. I'll be right back."

Lisa took the opportunity to visit the powder room to check her appearance. Her lipstick was fading and she hurriedly applied more. After smoothing the red across her lips, she was satisfied with what she saw and returned to the ballroom. Within seconds, Peter spotted her and attached himself to her side once more.

She wanted to mix and mingle by herself but couldn't do so with Peter shadowing her. She cared for Peter as a friend and didn't want to hurt him so she stayed with him and did her job.

She spotted Congressman Brogan and headed in his direction. They'd never met before, but he was attractive and affluent; she wanted a picture with him. Peter followed at her heels.

"Congressman Brogan," she greeted.

He looked at her with a confused expression. "Yes?"

"I'm Lisa Davenport, public relations assistant for the hotel." She extended her hand and he shook it.

"Very nice to meet you, Miss Davenport. You look lovely tonight," he replied.

After getting a picture with the Congressman and his constituents, she took Peter by the arm and ushered him toward a side staircase. She ascended a few steps to get a bird's-eye view of the crowd. When she spotted the First Family, she took Peter by the elbow and led him directly to the Nixons.

"How about a picture," she surprised Peter, and herself, when she addressed Mrs. Nixon and daughters, Tricia and Julie. Mrs. Nixon was wearing a shell-colored dress with matching gloves; Julie and Tricia wore elegant gowns and around their necks lay beautiful strands of pearls.

Mrs. Nixon politely smiled and nodded her consent. Lisa took her place between Julie and Tricia as though she were as prominent as the Nixons. Peter eyed the group through the lens. It was a perfect shot. He snapped the camera.

"Lisa Davenport!" came the scolding from a familiar voice.

Uh-oh. She turned to find her boss Christine approaching her in her signature black dress with diamond-studded, silver trim. She moved away from the First Family. No sense in them hearing the reprimand.

"Lisa Davenport, what were you thinking? You can't march up to the First Family and say 'How about a picture?' It's just not done!"

"Ms. Dubois!" Pearle called, sparing Lisa from the tongue-lashing.

Christine's scowl faded when Pearle joined them. "Ms. Mesta! How lovely to see you again."

With Christine locked into a conversation with Pearle, Lisa took the opportunity to slip away. What was so terribly wrong with asking the First Family for a picture? Christine was probably just jealous of Lisa's bold and vivacious personality. When Lisa wanted something, she wasn't afraid to go after it.

Peter didn't waste any time slipping away either. "Whew, that was a close call," he said while adjusting his bow tie. They moved to a quiet area in the ballroom to stand and observe. Peter took that opportunity to continue the conversation he'd started earlier.

"Lisa, do I have any qualities that you like in a man?"

Oh no, she thought. Not again. "Peter, you have several qualities that I like in a man."

"Then why are you marrying Brian? And don't say because you make a perfect couple."

"I really don't want to talk about this now." She was tired. "Come on, it's almost time to go."

"Just one more thing," he looked at her intently. "I don't want you to wake up one morning to find out you married a jerk."

The following morning, Lisa sat at the breakfast table in her apartment thinking about the changes that were taking place in her life. She loved Brian. She loved her job. Why couldn't she have both? Lisa placed her head on the table and began to cry.

Sandra, her perky twenty-four-year-old roommate, heard the noise and hurried to the kitchen.

Sandra and Lisa had been roommates and best friends for the past six years, since their freshman year at the University of

Maryland. Lisa had been an art history major, but dropped out after two years to earn some money to fund more college. When she got the job at the Sheraton Park Hotel she saw no reason to return to college. Besides, she would have had to give up wining and dining with senators and congressmen if she had chosen to return to school. The apartment the two shared was ideally located on Connecticut Avenue.

"Is there anything I can do to help?" Sandra asked.

"I don't know what to do!" Lisa sobbed. "I love Brian; he's attractive and successful. But I don't want to move in two months. *I don't want to move!*"

"Breathe," Sandra interjected.

"We barely have enough time to get married, go on a honeymoon, and move to Atlanta," she sighed. "I love my job; I don't want to leave. Everything's changing so fast." Sandra handed Lisa a Kleenex to wipe her tears.

"It's okay, Lisa," Sandra soothed. "You don't have to do anything you don't want to. Is Brian pushing you too fast?"

Lisa blinked back the tears. "Yes—but it's not just Brian. Last night, Peter told me he loved me."

Sandra smiled. "Peter's a wonderful guy. He's caring, and giving…more so than Brian is."

Lisa's head shot up. "What do you mean?"

Sandra thought for a moment then chose her words carefully. "Don't you think Brian can be a little…well, egocentric?"

Perhaps, Lisa thought to herself, but that's what made him such a catch. "Brian is a hunk. He carries himself well, cares about his appearance, drives a nice car, and takes me to the best restaurants."

"Do you really think those traits are enough to hold a marriage together?"

Lisa avoided the question. "He's so sweet and caring, but I don't love Peter."

Sandra smiled, wondering why Lisa chose to say *'I don't love Peter'* instead of *'I love Brian.'* Freud would have something to say about that, she thought. "I've always thought Peter was cute in his own unique way."

Lisa swirled the cream in her coffee and Sandra leaned over and put her arm around her. "I'll support you in whatever decision you make. But I will be very sad if you move. I'll never find another friend or roommate like you."

Chapter Two

Mr. and Mrs. Brian Caulder boarded Flight 1412 nonstop to Atlanta. Lisa immediately asked a flight attendant to hang her red velvet dress in first class. No way was she going to let that dress go through baggage, especially not since her New York flight fiasco when the airline lost her luggage. No one was going to lose this dress.

When they were situated in their seats, she looked at Brian. She still couldn't believe she was married. She absent-mindedly twirled the two-karat diamond ring on her finger.

The wedding had been beautiful. Most of her family was in attendance, except for her sister Marlene who was in Greece, and her father who passed away a few years earlier. A very old, dear friend walked her down the aisle and gave her away.

Their honeymoon had been quick, so quick that it seemed like a dream. They flew to the Bahamas and back in the blink of an eye. If it hadn't have been for the fact they had pictures, she'd question that they'd even been there. Upon their return, they hurriedly packed up their belongings and dashed to the airport to catch their flight to Atlanta.

As the plane accelerated down the runway, she gazed out the small, oval window, getting one last look at Washington. She was going to miss her home, her job, Sandra, the one person she was closest to, and Peter. She had invited him to attend the wedding, but understandably, he did not come. Her thoughts returned to the present when the flight attendant wheeled the beverage cart to their seats.

"Water, please," Lisa requested, remembering what Sandra once told her: *"Water will work miracles for your skin!"* She'd been right. Lisa drank at least eight glasses a day, if not more, and her olive complexion glowed.

"Scotch on the rocks with a twist of lemon," Brian requested.

Lisa gave him a disapproving look that he shrugged off. As far as she was concerned, he drank too much at times. When she would tell him so, he would withdraw. Well, at least Brian wasn't like her father who, although he had been a deeply religious man, would lose his temper at the drop of a hat. Her father had also been a hypocrite. He'd gone to church every Sunday, and forced her to go, but he rarely heard or lived by the words of the sermon. His faults created a deep void inside of her that left her continually yearning for outside validation. While growing up, no matter how hard she tried, she had never been able to please him.

The newlyweds set up housekeeping in a spacious three-bedroom condo in Atlanta that was close to Brian's office building, and many downtown hotels and restaurants. As Lisa was unpacking, Brian came up behind her and put his arms around her.

"I'm glad you're my wife and that you made this move with me. I know it was hard for you to give up your job," he announced. "You're the only person who seems to understand how important success is to me."

She turned around and threw her arms around him. "I do understand." That was all he ever talked about when they first started dating—success. He wanted to be powerful...rich. She had always admired his ambition; that was one of the reasons she was attracted to him in the first place.

He came from a poor family and that embarrassed him. His mother died when he was young and his father sank into a deep depression and began drinking. He was never successful in business and ended up working menial jobs that barely paid for the groceries each week. Brian was ashamed of his father and vowed he would never be like him. As far as he was concerned, his father was a failure.

When Brian graduated from high school, he enrolled at Georgetown University and worked to put himself through school. He promised himself that one day, he would wear the finest clothes, have the biggest house, drive the nicest car, and have a knockout for a wife. He once told her he had chosen her because she was the best. He'd known that every man who crossed her path in Washington wanted her; that's what made him want her all the more. She had dated high-profile men such as an ambassador, congressmen, and secret service men—all of them attractive and rich. Although Brian wasn't rich, he had a great job and could offer her security. He promised her that he would stay with her no matter what.

"You'll adjust, babe," Brian assured her. "You're fun, outgoing, and gorgeous. Who wouldn't want to hire you for a job? You'll make tons of friends just like you always do. Trust me, you made the right decision."

He always knew just what to say to make her feel good. She smiled and pulled him closer. "I saw an ad in the newspaper for a catering sales director at Bartonelli East. I think I'm going to apply tomorrow."

"That's great, honey. They'd be crazy not to hire you." He leaned down and brushed his lips against hers. The tender, soft kiss felt like heaven to her. How lucky was she? She had a wonderful husband and a beautiful, spacious condo. Now all she needed was a job like the one she had at the Sheraton Park. And a car. Maybe she would buy a BMW. She'd always dreamed of owning one.

The following day, Lisa walked into the lobby of Bartonelli East in the heart of downtown Atlanta. The hotel was breathtaking. The high ceiling revealed a glass elevator and a beautiful spiral staircase on either side of the check-in desk. The lobby was exquisite with its plush burgundy carpet and elegant furnishings. This was definitely what she was used to.

After inquiring about the position at the front desk, she was directed to the sales and catering office on the second floor. She ascended the stairs and upon finding no one seated in the reception area, she approached the inner office. There, she spied an attractive brunette sitting behind a mahogany desk. The nameplate on the desk read: *Vanessa Brimley, Catering Coordinator.*

She lightly tapped on the open door. The woman ignored her.

"Excuse me," Lisa spoke up. "I'm Lisa Caulder. I'm here to apply for the catering sales director position." She entered the office and offered her resume.

The woman made no effort to take Lisa's resume but instead informed, "The position's been filled."

"Oh, well. I just saw the ad yesterday and —"

"I said it's been filled," the woman snapped and returned to her work.

Lisa hoped the rest of Atlanta wasn't this rude. She placed her resume on the woman's desk. "Let me know if anything changes."

"It won't. But thanks anyway."

Disappointed, Lisa returned to the reception area where she paused briefly to cross off the hotel from her list of potential employers.

Arthur Brandon, General Manager of the hotel, watched the attractive, sharply dressed woman exit Vanessa's office. The soured expression on her face led him to believe that Vanessa was her rude self again, and may have cost him a potential client. If it weren't for the fact Vanessa was good in the sack, he would have fired her by now. He entered her office.

"Mr. Brandon, what can I do for you?" Vanessa asked in a seductive tone.

"What did that woman want?" he asked.

"She was looking for a job. I reviewed her resume," she lied, "and she is under-qualified, so I sent her away. I didn't want to bother you."

"Vanessa," he scolded, "I told you to send *all* applicants to my office. I know you want that job, but Mr. Bartonelli wants me to interview all new prospects."

"Sorry, Arthur," she pouted. "It won't happen again. Are we still on for tonight?"

"Shh! Damn, Vanessa, keep your voice down." He leaned down and whispered into her ear. "Yes. My office. Eight o'clock."

Brian pulled his car into the condo parking lot. He opened the car door and hopped out whistling a happy tune. Life was grand. He had his dream job *and* his dream girl. Once he saved a little more money, he'd have a nicer house and flashier car, too. To him, the more material possessions he owned meant the more respected he would be.

He smelled dinner cooking as soon as he entered the condo. He paused briefly in the hallway to listen as his wife sang along with Elton John's *Don't Let the Sun Go Down on Me* that was playing on the radio. She had a beautiful voice and he liked it when she sang. When he entered the kitchen, she was removing her famous Chicken Royal casserole from the oven. He watched her in silence for a moment then crept up behind her."

"I am the luckiest man alive," he whispered into her ear.

Startled, Lisa jumped but managed to hold on to the casserole. She carefully placed it on the trivet then threw a dish towel at him. "You scared me half to death!"

He caught the towel and Lisa embraced him warmly. "I'm the lucky one."

Brian stared at her with a boyish grin on his face.

"What's that look for?" she asked.

"Gorgeous…and can cook, too. Quite a package I've got," he beamed.

"Well, I'm still learning."

"To look good or cook?" he teased.

"Both."

While she finished preparing the meal, he set the table. Yes, this was the life he had always dreamed of. It was perfect. He was successful and she was successful. So what if she hadn't gotten the job as catering sales director. Tomorrow was another day and with her charm and beauty, there was no doubt she'd be snatched up soon.

He remembered the first time they'd met. They were both living in the same apartment building. He watched her unload groceries wearing hot pants. She was a knockout. He knew at that point he wanted her. She played hard to get at first, but over time, his persistence paid off. It always had.

Lisa knew he was staring at her, admiring her, and she surprised them both when she asked, "You'd still adore me if I was frumpy, wouldn't you?" She wasn't sure where the question came from, it just sort of came out before she had time to think about it.

"Huh?" It took him a second to understand what she was asking. He laughed when he did. "Babe, that would never happen to you. You're beautiful. You're perfect," he assured her. "Now, come sit down so we can eat this fabulous dinner."

She smiled and was just about to sit down next to him when the phone rang. She ran to get it.

"Hello?"

"Hello, Mrs. Caulder?"

"Yes, this is Lisa Caulder."

"This is Arthur Brandon, General Manager of Bartonelli East." He peered outside his office to make sure Vanessa was finally gone for the night after their rendezvous. She was.

"Hello, Mr. Brandon. How are you?"

"I'm fine. I, uh, I came across the resume you dropped off earlier today and I must say I'm impressed with your credentials. I see you worked in the catering office at Bartonelli, Capitol Hill. I also see that you have some experience in catering as well as public relations at the Sheraton Park, working under Christine Dubois."

Lisa perked up. "Yes, that's correct."

"I think you would be perfect as our new catering sales director and I'd like you to come in for an interview. We had someone on the inside vying for the promotion, but I am very impressed with your experience, Mrs. Caulder. Would you be available to meet with me on Monday at, say, ten?"

"That would be wonderful," she replied. "Thank you, Mr. Brandon. I look forward to meeting with you on Monday at ten."

"Great. See you then." Arthur hung up the phone, pleased with himself. *Vanessa may be qualified for a romp in the sack, but not for this position.*

Later that evening, Brian crawled between the ivory satin sheets and patiently waited for his wife to emerge from the oversized bathroom and join him in bed. The sheets were her favorite; that's why he'd purchased them for her while on their honeymoon. He reached over and fiddled with the clock radio trying to find the perfect station to put her into a romantic mood. He settled on a soft jazz station.

She finally emerged from the bathroom wearing a black satin nightgown that he'd picked up on a business trip. Each time he went out of town, he never failed to surprise her with some type of gift or trinket upon his return. He loved to spoil her and she loved to be spoiled. He watched her comb out her long, dark brown hair.

"You become more beautiful every day, Lisa," he told her.

She smiled seductively before crawling beneath the sheet. He immediately showered her with kisses.

"You certainly know how to make a woman feel special," she purred.

He pulled her close and gave her another warm kiss before reaching over to turn off the lamp. The moonlight streamed through the opening of the drapes and he decided to take advantage of it. He moved away from her.

"Where are you going?" she asked.

He opened the drapes further and the moonlight filled the room with a soft glow. She was completely visible to him.

"I want to see your beautiful face while we make love," was the last thing he said before they expressed their love to each other.

Chapter Three

On Monday morning, Brian pulled into Bartonelli East to pick up his wife after her interview. He crossed his fingers that she got the job. As he entered the catering office, he was surprised to be greeted by a sexy woman wearing a red dress that was perhaps a bit too short to be considered office attire. But he couldn't take his eyes off her shapely legs.

"Yes?" Vanessa asked, well aware he was looking at her legs and not her eyes.

Brian's head snapped up. "I'm here to pick up Lisa Caulder. Do you know if she's out of her interview yet?"

"She's still in the interview. And you are..."

"Brian. Brian Caulder—her husband."

She rounded her desk to stand before him and shook his hand. So, this handsome man was Lisa's husband.

"Nice to meet you, Brian Caulder," she seductively replied. "I'm Vanessa Brimley, catering coordinator." She licked her upper lip, which he missed due to the fact he was checking out her voluptuous figure.

"Brian!" Lisa called from just outside the office. She had seen Vanessa flirt with her husband as she left the interview and it made her blood boil.

"Hey, babe, how'd it go?" he asked.

She momentarily forgot her jealousy and smiled. "I got the job!"

Brian embraced her. "I'm so proud of you, babe. This calls for a celebration. We have my company's banquet to attend tonight, but we'll go out tomorrow evening and celebrate over a romantic dinner." He kissed her on the lips.

Take that, Vanessa, Lisa thought to herself as she wrapped her arms around Brian's neck and returned the kiss melting into his arms.

When the kiss was over, she announced, "I have to go to Personnel and fill out some forms, but when I'm done, I want to show you my new office. You can wait here, if you like. I'll be right back."

Lisa was no sooner out of the office that Vanessa rounded her desk and boldly slipped her business card into Brian's back pocket.

"Just in case you ever need a catering coordinator, my home number is on the back."

As she waltzed by him, he was taken aback by her forwardness. But he also was mesmerized by her sway as she continued down the hall. He pulled the card out of his pocket, stared at it for a moment, smiled, and slipped it back into his pocket.

Later that evening, as the two dressed for the banquet, Brian was excited about the black tie affair where he would meet the company's new executive team, and impress everyone with his trophy wife.

Lisa slipped into her red velvet dress and Brian seductively eyed her. "How did I get so lucky?"

"Well, Mr. Caulder," she smiled coyly. "It's because you're so handsome."

She turned her back to him and lifted her hair out of the way. "Can you?" she asked, indicating her need for help with the zipper. He reached over and easily glided the zipper up to the beaded collar. After she applied her makeup, the two were out the door.

Lisa remained at her husband's side most of the night while his colleagues doted over him. A couple of times, he ventured out on his own and she felt somewhat uncomfortable.

"Hey babe," he returned to her side with another couple. "I want you to meet Stuart and Angie Lyons. Stuart does advertising for the company. We spent the past week working together."

Lisa shook hands with Stuart and Angie then the four sat down to dinner.

"Angie, what do you do?" Lisa asked.

"I'm a high school teacher," she replied. "I enjoy working with teenagers. I've been doing it since my sister was paralyzed in an automobile collision."

Angie missed the soured expression on Stuart's face at the mention of the collision, but Lisa didn't.

"That's horrible, Angie. I'm so sorry to hear that. How did it happen?" Lisa prodded.

"Drunk driver," she softly replied. She lowered her gaze for a moment then looked up and forced a smile. "Look at me, depressing everyone. Let's change the subject." She turned to

Lisa. "I know that you're new in town and you probably haven't met very many people yet. Would you like to join me for lunch someday, and maybe play a game of tennis?"

"I would love to," she replied. "I enjoy tennis."

"Is that how you maintain your trim figure?" Angie asked.

Lisa smiled. "Yes, I exercise so I can eat whatever I want."

"You're lucky," Angie replied. "If I even *look* at dessert, I gain weight." She wished she could be as petite as Lisa. After she married Stuart, her weight increased and she seemed to have no control over it. And the fact that Stuart was always reminding her of it didn't help matters much. Angie knew that Stuart had always dated knockouts before her; she also knew he'd had several affairs during their marriage. She chose to look the other way.

Lisa immediately liked Angie. She was attractive in a unique sort of way with her short, curly auburn hair and vibrant green eyes. Stuart, medium height with dark brown hair, had a goatee that made him look more distinguished than he probably deserved. He was still physically fit after ten years of marriage and was a bit on the arrogant side. But why shouldn't he be? He was well known in the community and was wealthy. He was the life of the party and always kept everyone laughing.

Brian turned the black Ford Taurus into the parking lot of the hotel and kissed Lisa good-bye. "Have a good first day at your new job, babe."

"I will," she smiled. She couldn't wait to start the day.

Vanessa had been looking out her office window when the car pulled up to the hotel. She felt a pang of jealousy when she saw the newlyweds kiss good-bye.

Stacey, a co-worker, entered the office and placed the nameplate *Lisa Caulder, Catering Sales Director* on the mahogany desk; she spied Vanessa looking out the window. Glancing over Vanessa's shoulder, she saw what held the woman's attention.

"Would you stop gawking at our new boss and help me for a minute?"

Vanessa jumped. "Could you not sneak up on me like that?"

Stacey moved to get a better view of the newlyweds saying their good-byes. "You'd think our new boss could at least be on time."

Vanessa's catty expression deepened. "Now, now, Stacey. Be on your best behavior."

"Hah! Listen to you," Stacey shot back. "You dislike her more than I do."

"You're right, I do," Vanessa agreed. "Who wouldn't? She's beautiful, sexy, and has a great job...a job *I* was supposed to get!" She lowered her voice. "And she's married to an extremely attractive man."

"Much as I dislike her, I have to admit she is more qualified for the job than you are."

Vanessa scowled. "Whose side are you on anyway?"

Stacey thought for a moment. If she had to have an enemy on the job, she'd much rather it was Lisa. Lisa was harmless compared to the chaos Vanessa could create if she didn't like someone.

"Yours," Stacey replied. "Anyway, I think you're more upset that she's got that hunk of a husband than you are that she got your job."

Stacey was right—he was a catch.

Vanessa retrieved some folders and began aimlessly shuffling through them; giving the appearance she was hard at work. When Lisa entered the office, Vanessa put on her happy face.

"Lisa, welcome aboard," Vanessa greeted. "I'd like you to meet Stacey."

"It's nice to meet you," Stacey said and stepped forward to give her a hug. Lisa knew it was an empty gesture, but she returned the hug anyway.

"Thank you."

"You're new desk is ready, Mrs. Caulder," Stacey said, pointing to the desk with Lisa's nameplate.

"Wonderful," Lisa replied. "You know, I'm still not used to being called Mrs. Caulder."

"We'll say it so many times, you'll get used to it in no time," Stacey replied with a nervous laugh.

Lisa stepped around the two and entered her plush new office. She sat at her desk. "Vanessa, can you come in for a moment?"

Vanessa rolled her eyes but did as Lisa requested. "Yes?"

"I think the first thing we should do is pull the files of all the companies that have had banquets here in the past few years. I'd like to get in touch with them, introduce myself, and hopefully get an appointment. Can you have them on my desk within the hour?"

"No problem. Will that be all?" she asked aloud, but finished with *"your highness"* in her mind.

"For the moment."

Lisa looked up from shuffling through papers on her desk and noted Vanessa's scowl. Well, Vanessa would just have to get used to the fact Lisa was in charge and she was working for her! "That'll be all."

Lisa and Brian spent the evening dining at the Blue Olive Restaurant with Angie and Stuart. The four were becoming fast friends as far as Lisa was concerned. She was especially fond of Angie and liked spending time with her. The fact that Angie didn't feel threatened by Lisa's looks was a rarity. She felt comfortable in Angie's presence and welcomed her companionship, whether they were shopping, having lunch, or playing tennis. Angie was a giving person and Lisa admired and respected her. The guys had bonded, too. They had football and drinking in common. There was also a competitiveness about them that centered on their love of money and materialism.

Spending time with Stuart and Angie also served to take her mind off work. She was constantly at odds with Vanessa who tried as hard as she could to make Lisa's job difficult. Lisa was able to pinpoint the many times Vanessa had tried to sabotage her work; it was the times she didn't know about that concerned her.

Lisa sat at her desk shuffling through the papers in an attempt to get caught up. The phone rang again; it had been ringing all morning. She had been at her job for almost a year now and was confident in her position.

"Catering office, this is Lisa," she grabbed it on the first ring.

"Lisa, it's Arthur Brandon. I have a problem—actually an emergency. I need you in my office immediately."

"I'll be right there," she replied, wondering what put the edge in his voice this morning.

She entered his office and found him pacing. "I can't believe this, Lisa," he said.

"What's wrong?"

"The Maharajah and his entourage are scheduled to arrive in two days."

"Yes, I'm aware of that," she replied.

"Someone in your department dropped the ball when they didn't take his special diet requirements into consideration."

Figures. That task was assigned to Vanessa. Lisa kept her cool. "What are the requirements?"

"Fifty pounds of basmati rice," he replied, the beads of sweat clearly visible on his forehead.

Lisa crossed to his desk and picked up the phone. She dialed a number and placed the call on speakerphone.

"House of Partukah," came the thick East Indian accent.

"Hello. This is Lisa Caulder, Catering Sales Director at Bartonelli East in Atlanta. We have an account with you."

"Yes, this is true, Ms. Lisa. What may I be doing for you on this day?"

"We inadvertently overlooked the special diet requirements of the Maharajah who will be staying with us and we need fifty pounds of basmati rice by tomorrow."

"This is a lot of rice on a very short notice," he replied.

"Yes, it is, and I apologize for that," Lisa offered. "Can you help us out?"

The phone was silent for a moment. "For you, pretty lady, I will have the rice to you."

Lisa smiled and her boss relaxed and wiped the sweat from his brow. "Thank you," she replied then added, "If I remember correctly, you're a Hawks fan, right?"

"You remember. Yes! Yes!"

"We have two extra tickets for this weekend's game. I'll see that they are sent to you today."

Lisa brought the call to a close and looked at Arthur. The bewildered look on his face told her that he was both impressed with her handling of the situation, and embarrassed that he'd lost his cool under pressure, while she maintained hers. Regardless, he had total confidence in her abilities and knew he'd made the right decision in hiring her.

Chapter Four

That weekend, Lisa and Brian planned a picnic outing with Angie and Stuart. The four were just preparing to leave the condo when the phone rang. Brian ran back to answer it. The pained expression on his face as he handed the phone off to Lisa conveyed it couldn't be good news.

"It's Vanessa," he mouthed.

"Hello, Vanessa," she spoke. As she listened to the woman on the other end, her expression soured. "I'm sorry you're sick." More silence, followed by a frown. "Yes, I'll cover for you today."

Brian, Angie, and Stuart groaned in unison.

Lisa hung up the phone and explained that Vanessa wasn't feeling well and she would need to cover for her today, at least until noon. She promised she would join them at the lake when she got off. The group walked her to her new silver BMW and Brian gave her a hug before she got in and drove off.

Kelly Brannigan and Cathy Wallace exited the doors of the ten-story hospital and inhaled the crisp morning air. It was refreshing, but did nothing to rejuvenate them. Both women had spent the entire night working in the intensive care unit.

"Thanks for giving me a ride home," Cathy said before yawning.

"No problem," Kelly replied. She was always willing to help a friend, and Cathy was not only her friend, she was her protégé.

They had no sooner pulled onto the main road when Kelly looked over and saw Cathy was asleep. Kelly couldn't wait until she got home and her head hit the pillow. The drive to Cathy's house would take her a distance out of her way, but she didn't mind.

As she drove along a stretch of open road, her mind wandered. She rolled her window down hoping the cool air would keep her awake. She had no sooner put her hand back on the steering wheel when a Chevy Malibu came out of nowhere and almost hit the driver's side of her car. She immediately snapped to and swerved her vehicle to avoid the collision. She laid on the horn and the driver of the Malibu fell in behind her, nearly rear-ending her.

Cathy woke up just in time to see the Malibu try to pass them a second time. It finally sped by, but its driver failed to return to his lane after he cleared her car. He continued driving on the wrong side of the road.

"Jerk!" Kelly spat. "What's wrong with that idiot?"

"Whew, he must be crazy." Cathy sat up and reflexively tightened her seat belt.

"More like drunk if you ask me," Kelly countered. "Just look at that!"

The Malibu continued on the wrong side of the road and oncoming traffic was forced to swerve right and left to avoid hitting it.

"Someone needs to call the police," Kelly said.

The Malibu began to climb a hill in the road, still on the wrong side. Kelly prayed no one was approaching from the other side.

Lisa drove up the hill, singing along to *Lucy in the Sky with Diamonds* playing on the radio. Life doesn't get any better than this, she thought. She had a successful husband, a wonderful condo, a great job, and an awesome car. Those were her last thoughts before everything went black…

Kelly screamed when she saw the Malibu plow into another vehicle that was cresting the hill from the opposite direction.

"Oh, God!" Cathy cried.

Kelly sped up to the scene and brought her vehicle to a screeching halt. As the two women exited their vehicle, they watched a man stumble from the mangled Malibu. He was cursing and holding his head.

"Wh-what…the hell's goin' on here anyhow," he slurred.

Kelly sidestepped the driver of the Malibu, and ran to the mangled silver car that no longer looked like a car but instead a crushed tin can.

She looked inside and cringed at the gruesome scene. A young woman, restrained by her seatbelt, was unresponsive. Her face had been smashed in by the steering wheel. Blood was oozing from her mouth and ears. Not a good sign. Kelly tried to climb into the vehicle from the passenger's side.

The driver of a semi witnessed the accident and pulled his rig to the side of the road. He exited the cab and ran over to help.

"We need to get her out," Kelly told him. "I don't think she's breathing."

While Cathy, the truck driver, and Kelly worked to free the woman from the mangled metal, traffic began to back up on both lanes. Other motorists exited their vehicles and came to offer assistance to the three. Finally, the young woman was freed from the wreckage.

They gently placed her body on the ground and Kelly was unable to detect a pulse. She tried to clear the woman's airway, but it was a difficult task since her face was shattered. She gave her a few quick breaths. No response. She tried again. This time, the unconscious woman began to breathe on her own.

Cathy stood up and shouted to anyone, "Call an ambulance! Somebody call for an ambulance!"

By this time an officer had arrived on the scene and placed the call. While the two nurses worked to stabilize the woman, the officer approached the driver of the Malibu. The man, Walter Fowler, had only a few minor injuries…and he was clearly drunk. The officer could smell the liquor on his breath but needed to administer a blood test for the record. He called for a second ambulance although he thought the man did not deserve one.

The trauma team was ready for the young female victim as the ambulance backed up to the emergency entrance at Northridge Hospital. They immediately wheeled her critically injured body into the emergency room where Dr. George Clayton, a young doctor in his late-twenties, began calling out directives. The woman's body was transferred from the gurney onto the exam table and several sensing devices were immediately hooked up to her body. The trauma team went to work assessing her injuries.

"Damn it! We're about to lose her," Dr. Clayton warned at one point. "Paddles now!"

A trauma nurse prepared the electrical paddles and handed them off to Dr. Clayton. He positioned them on the dying woman and yelled, "Clear!" before sending the electric current through her body. The oscilloscope continued to show a straight line.

"Again. Clear!" He zapped her again. Still no change. It wasn't until he sent the current through her body a third time that the oscilloscope measured a faint heartbeat. The trauma team resumed their work.

The young woman was far from being out of danger, but at least she was momentarily stabilized. Her face, bluish-black in color, was swollen to twice its normal size and looked anything but human. Gone were all the physical features that made this woman who she was. She was unrecognizable—her beautiful face was gone...

Brian, Angie, and Stuart were fishing from the sailboat on the lake when Brian looked off in the distance and said, "She should have been here by now."

"Maybe we should go ashore, Stuart," Angie suggested, sensing Brian's worry.

Stuart shifted the sail and they headed back to the dock. Once there, Brian stepped off the boat and scanned the parking area and the other docks. There was no sign of Lisa. He reached into his pocket and pulled out some coins and headed to the pay phone to call the hotel.

Arthur answered the phone and when Brian asked to speak to Lisa, he expressed his frustration that Lisa had not shown up for work yet. While Arthur continued with his tirade, Brian became panicked. Where was his beautiful Lisa?

Next he called their condo and his anxiety intensified when their answering machine picked up. After the beep, he called out, "Lisa, if you're there, pick up. Lisa? Pick up." Nothing. His gut churned. Something was wrong.

Angie and Stuart arrived at the phone booth just as he slammed the receiver down on the hook.

"Have you reached her yet?" Angie asked.

"She's not at home or at work," he replied, his voice faltering. "I need to go look for her." His insides ached. What could have happened to her?

He raced over to his car and heard Angie call out, "Let us know when you find her, Brian. Call us and let us know everything's all right!"

Stuart saw the fear in his wife's eyes and he pulled her into his embrace. "It's probably nothing, Angie."

Brian pulled into the condo parking lot and didn't miss the police officer exiting the building. He tried to swallow the lump forming in his throat. He willed himself to get out of the car.

The officer looked at him. "Are you Brian Caulder?"

Brian's knees buckled. "Yes."

"Mr. Caulder, I'm sorry to have to tell you this, but your wife has been in a serious automobile accident."

"Oh, God." He placed his hand on the hood of his car to steady himself.

"She was hit by an oncoming car on Spring Road. She's in the ICU at Northridge Hospital."

"Is…is she all right?" He broke into a sweat.

The officer lowered his gaze. "Mr. Caulder, she's stabilized for the time being. But you need to get down there right away."

"Yes—yes," he acknowledged.

"If you'd like, I can drive you," the officer offered.

"No. No, I'll leave right now."

Brian didn't wait for the officer to respond. He hopped into his car and sped out of the parking lot. His mind raced a mile a minute and he was having a difficult time remaining calm. His heart was beating fast and his insides were churning. What if she was dying and he couldn't get to her in time? What if she was already dead?

What was wrong with him? The officer was mistaken. It couldn't be Lisa. She was probably at the hotel right now working. There was a mix-up. There had to be a mix-up. He would go to the hospital anyway and let them know they had made a mistake.

He entered Northridge and went to the front desk. "I'm Brian Caulder. I think there's been a mistake. I was told that my wife is in intensive care, but that can't be."

The woman behind the desk shuffled through some papers. "Is your wife's name Lisa Caulder?"

"Yes."

"Mr. Caulder, your wife *is* in ICU. Follow me, please."

He followed the nurse to the ICU where he was met by a doctor.

"Mr. Caulder, I'm Dr. Clayton."

The young doctor reached out to shake Brian's hand but Brian didn't extend his own. He was in shock. It finally sunk in that it wasn't a mix-up. His wife *was* in the ICU.

"Where is she?" he hurriedly asked. "I want to see my wife! Where is my wife!"

"Mr. Caulder," the doctor ushered him into a small room where they would have some privacy. "Your wife is in the intensive care unit—she's alive. That's all I can tell you right now, other than it's a miracle that she is still alive. We're still running tests but I suspect brain damage, and possible blindness."

Brian's concentration was fading in and out.

"She's on life support right now; her brain can't control her vitals at this point," he paused to give the young man some time to absorb all the bad news he was telling him.

"Her face hit the steering wheel; all of her facial bones are broken. Her injuries are severe, Mr. Caulder." He reached into his pocket and retrieved two rings. "We took these off her finger."

Brian took the diamond ring and the wedding band from the doctor's palm. They were Lisa's. It was really her.

"I want to see her now!"

"You can see her, Mr. Caulder," the doctor replied. "But I want to caution you that you won't recognize her. She suffered extensive facial damage."

Brian swayed and the doctor reached out to steady him.

"I can handle it," Brian replied and backed away. "I want to see her."

Dr. Clayton walked him to the ICU. There, the trauma nurse led him to his wife's bedside. They rounded a canopied area and he came face to face with Lisa's broken body.

"Oh, God," he sobbed when he saw her condition. Her entire head was swollen and her once-beautiful chestnut brown eyes were swollen shut. Tightly drawn stitches hinted at where her mouth and nose were. There was a small gap near her mouth and he saw that some of her teeth were in disarray.

He was horrified. His knees buckled again and everything went black around him until the smelling salt was placed under his nose. His head shot up and his mind quickly cleared. Dr. Clayton helped him from the room.

"Sh-she doesn't look human."

"The impact was so violent her facial bone structure was pulverized," the doctor said.

"It-it can be fixed, right?" Brian asked, hopeful. "You can make her look like she did before, can't you?"

"Fixed, no," the doctor responded. "Possibly restored." He placed his hand on Brian's shoulder and genuinely added, "I'm sorry."

Brian snapped. "Where's the son of a bitch that did this to her!"

The doctor took hold of his arm to prevent him from tearing through the hospital. "That's not going to help your wife, Mr. Caulder. Let's take care of her first and we can worry about him later."

Brian came to his senses and nodded. Lisa. He had to focus on Lisa.

Brian made the necessary calls to friends and relatives before settling down in Lisa's room for the night. He dozed off a couple of times even though the chair was uncomfortable. By morning, he looked a mess. His hair was matted and his eyes were bloodshot. He heard the ding of the elevator and the familiar voices when the doors opened. It was Faith Davenport, Lisa's mother, and Lisa's younger sister Diana.

He met them in the hallway. Faith took one look at him and immediately started crying. He hugged her and blinked back his own tears. No one said a word for a moment.

Diana wiped away her tears and asked, "Brian, how did it happen?"

"Drunk driver. If I ever get my hands on that son of a—"

"I want to see my daughter," Faith said and took hold of Brian's arm for support.

"Faith," he blinked back more tears. "She doesn't look like you remember. She looks bad...really bad."

"Thank you, Brian, but I want to see her."

Brian led the two to Lisa's bedside where Kelly Brannigan, the trauma nurse, was checking her vitals.

"You can visit for a few moments," Kelly said before leaving the room.

Faith gasped when she saw her daughter's distorted face. She took her daughter's hand in hers and leaned over to kiss her bruised and swollen face as only a mother could. "Oh God, Lisa, what happened to you?"

Diana took one look at her sister and fainted.

Later that evening, Faith took over Lisa's kitchen and prepared Chicken Royal, a recipe that had been in the family for years. She knew it was one of Brian's favorite dishes—that's why she had chosen to make it.

She felt helpless and it made her very uncomfortable. She'd spent most of her life being in control, and being the foundation for everyone else. She was a rock and always managed to hold things together no matter how bad the situation. But this was out of her league. She had no control over Lisa's condition and she hated the fact.

She called Brian and Diana to the table when the meal was ready.

The three sat quietly. There was no conversation, just the sound of the serving spoon clanking against the bowl as portions were doled out.

Diana looked at her mother across the table. Normally, under strained conditions, her mother could be heard saying, "There's nothing a bowl of chicken soup won't fix!" It had been her motto for years. Diana needed to hear her mother say that now. But the words never came.

Faith didn't miss the fear in her daughter's eyes. She forced a smile hoping to ease Diana's worry. She looked at Brian; he was playing with the broccoli on his plate. No one seemed to have an appetite.

Faith's thoughts turned to the long road that would be ahead for her daughter — *if she came out of the coma*. She knew Lisa's appearance played an important role in her life. And whether it was right or wrong, she knew her daughter based her worth on her looks. Everyone always told Lisa "You're so pretty," or "What beautiful eyes." Rarely did anyone acknowledge her accomplishments. Faith sometimes saw Lisa's pained expression when her sister Marlene was praised for her piano playing, or when Chad was lauded for playing the guitar. Randy was often complimented for his singing, and, of course, Diana was known for always receiving straight A's. All anyone praised Lisa for was her looks.

"Momma," Diana broke the silence. "I don't feel like eating." She rose from her seat and gave Brian a sisterly hug. "What if Lisa never comes out of the coma?"

He pulled away from her. "I don't want to think like that. She'll be all right. She has to be."

Faith's eyes came to rest on a framed photograph of Brian and Lisa sitting on the buffet. It had been taken while the two were on their honeymoon. Lisa's smile was wide and she looked happy. She would never look like that again.

"My baby, my baby," Faith cried, giving in to the tears. "The only part of her I recognized in the hospital were her hands!"

"Momma, don't cry," Diana pleaded. She'd never seen her mother fall apart and she didn't know what to do. She ran from the room.

Faith pushed her plate away. "I'm sorry, Brian. I can't sit here and eat when I don't even know if my daughter is going to live." She left the room and ascended the steps to the guestroom. She would pray—it was all that she could do.

Brian sat alone in the dining room feeling more alone than he ever had in his life. "Why God? Why Lisa?" He slammed his fist to the table.

Later that evening, he returned to the hospital where he held a vigil throughout the night at Lisa's bedside. He would never forgive the drunk driver who did this to her.

The following days were a blur. No one got much sleep or ate very much, and there was still no response from Lisa. Stuart and Angie stopped by the ICU every day to offer their prayers and support.

On the fifth day, Faith leaned down to kiss her daughter's bruised and swollen face when she arrived, as she did every day, and was surprised and excited to see Lisa's eye twitch.

"She moved!" Faith cried out to anyone within earshot. "Honey, it's Momma. Can you hear me?"

Nothing.

"Lisa, can you hear me?"

Lisa's eyes twitched again and eventually fluttered open.

Faith squealed. "Lisa! Look at me!"

Lisa blinked a couple of times, as though she was trying to clear her vision.

"Lisa, can you see me? What color am I wearing?" Faith continued coaxing a response from her daughter.

"Green." came the soft, strained reply.

Faith looked at her outfit. It *was* green! "Oh thank God!"

Brian and Diana rounded the corner to the room in time to hear Lisa's voice.

"Nurse! Doctor! Anybody!" Brian shouted into the hallway. "She's awake!" His heart raced and for the first time in days, he was hopeful.

Faith began sobbing and kissing her daughter's face.

The room quickly filled with medical personnel and was abuzz with activity. One of the nurses checking Lisa's vital signs smiled at her. "Your husband is here, honey."

"I-I d-don't have a husband," Lisa whispered, confused.

The nurse noticed the hurt expression on Brian's face. She reached over and touched his arm. "You've been married such a short time; she probably doesn't remember that yet."

Dr. Clayton entered the room and Brian, Faith, and Diana were ushered out.

Chapter Five

Brian and Faith held hands tightly as Dr. Clayton led them into one of the small conference rooms. He gestured for the two to take a seat. Brian hated this room. It was the same room where he'd first learned of Lisa's injuries. A team of doctors entered the room next and introductions were made.

Dr. Warrington, a neurologist, spoke first. "Lisa has brain damage. We won't know the extent until we run some tests."

Brian stiffened.

Dr. Traynor, an ophthalmologist spoke next. "We believe that Lisa will be permanently blind in her left eye. The optic nerve was completely severed."

"But is she out of danger?" Faith asked.

"We're still running tests. But the fact that she came out of the coma is a good sign," Dr. Clayton answered.

"What about her face?" Brian asked. "Will it heal?"

Dr. Howden, the plastic surgeon, spoke up. "Lisa has a set of fractures to her facial bones as bad as anyone I have ever seen survive. She's fortunate to be alive. Even if corrective surgery is possible, she will never look the same."

The room fell silent. Brian sank back into his chair trying to digest everything.

"*If?* What do you mean *if?*" he finally asked.

Dr. Howden explained that Lisa's facial bones were pulverized—like powder.

"The skeletal structure of her face will have to be completely rebuilt before we can even think about trying to make her look like a young woman again."

"I don't understand. What does that mean?" Brian asked.

"She was hit so hard that her face broke away from her skull," Dr. Howden replied. "The first thing we need to do before we even consider plastic surgery is to schedule a cleanup operation—today, if possible. You'll need to sign consent forms before we can proceed."

Within a short amount of time, Lisa was wheeled into surgery. Brian decided he would do his waiting sitting on the steps outside the hospital. The sun was shining and the sky was clear. He watched a bird soar overhead and wished he could trade places with it. He wanted to fly away from all his problems.

He thought about the dreams he and Lisa had shared. Would they ever be realized? Would things ever be the same? He just wanted everything to go back to normal.

Inside the operating room, Lisa lay on the operating table breathing through the hole cut in her trachea. A long tube extended from the hole into an oxygen supply to help her breathe easier. Dr. Howden began picking tiny bone fragments out of her face, one by one.

"Her jaw is broken in three places," he assessed. "We'll need a wire placement."

He carefully implanted the metal wires to attach her skull to her skin. When he was done, they protruded out of her head and looked like small antennas.

Brian returned to the OR waiting area and began pacing. Stuart and Angie looked at each other and wished they could do or say something that would make him stop worrying.

Stuart got a cup of coffee from the vending machine. "Here," he handed the cup to Brian. "Drink this."

"Thanks, man." Brian took the cup.

"We're here for you, Brian, you know that right?" Stuart said. He hated dealing with emotions, but he figured Brian needed to hear the words.

"Yea."

Angie joined them. "Brian, this probably isn't the time or place to bring this up, but I think you should talk to an attorney." She handed him the business card of a personal injury attorney. "He lives across the street from us."

Brian looked at the card and put it into his pocket. He'd deal with that later.

Six hours later, Lisa's surgery was complete. When she came out of the anesthesia, she was confused and tried to remove the tracheotomy tube that was preventing her from speaking. The nurse tried to sooth her and explained that the tube needed to remain for now. But she would be able to talk when it was removed.

Lisa wasn't soothed. She frantically pulled at the tube and it took two nurses to hold her down. They tied her hands to the bed until she calmed down. They brought Brian in to help calm her. When they finally released her hands, she grabbed the notepad and pencil and began scrawling a message.

"Something's wrong with me. I need to be in the hospital!" she wrote.

"You are in the hospital, babe," he soothed.

She didn't understand. She was confused. She couldn't talk. She needed help. Who were all these people? The thoughts raced through her mind and she tried to make sense of it all.

The day nurse entered the room and asked Brian to step out while she checked her vitals. She was terse with him and he immediately didn't like her, but he obeyed her request and left the room.

After checking her vitals, the nursed tried to drag a comb through Lisa's long hair, but it was matted and caked with dried blood.

"We need to do something about this hair," the nurse spoke. She reached for a pair of scissors and Lisa's eyes widened and she began to struggle against the nurse, but she was too weak to fight and finally gave up. The nurse cut Lisa's once-beautiful long hair up to her chin. Tears filled her eyes and streamed down her cheeks. She still didn't fully understand what was going on—but she knew her hair was gone.

"There we go. Much better," the nurse praised her work before leaving the room.

When Brian entered the room a few moments later, he took one look at Lisa's cropped hair and cursed.

"Lisa, what happened to your hair?"

She put pen to paper and angrily scribbled, "THE NURSE CUT IT!"

Brian stormed out of the room and went to the nurse's station. "Where's the nurse who cut my wife's hair?" he yelled.

The day nurse squared her shoulders and replied, "I cut it. It was matted and there was no way I was going to comb out that mess every day. It was a nuisance and it needed to be cut."

Brian came within an inch of her face. "Don't you *ever* cut my wife's hair again! Do you understand me?"

The nurse backed away from him. "I'm just doing my job."

"Well, the next time you do your job in my wife's room, you check with me or her mother before you *ever* do anything that changes her appearance!"

Was this man blind the nurse wondered? Good Lord, the woman's appearance changed more in the blink of an eye during the crash than it would in her lifetime.

Brian didn't wait for her response. He returned to Lisa's room and awkwardly put his arms around her. With all the equipment she was hooked up to, it made the task difficult.

He rocked her gently while her tears continued to fall; he didn't know what else to do.

Faith sat by her daughter's bedside and smoothed Lisa's short hair away from her face. It had been a month since the drunk driver plowed into Lisa's car.

Her mouth was still wired shut, but she was able to talk. Eating was difficult, but Faith would sit by her side at mealtime and encourage her. Usually, Lisa dribbled more soup down her chin than she got into her mouth. Faith wanted to jump in and feed Lisa herself, but the nurses had talked her out of it; it was better to let Lisa learn how to do it on her own. Faith reluctantly agreed.

Today was an especially sad day for Lisa; Faith and Diana were flying home. She wanted them to stay.

Diana entered the room with their suitcases. "Mom, we need to get going if we're going to catch our flight." She eased the suitcases to the floor and hugged Lisa. "I love you, sis."

Faith hugged her next. "Sweetheart, I don't want to leave, but I have to. I need to get back to your brothers. You'll be going home tomorrow and Brian will take good care of you." She kissed her on the forehead. "We'll pray for you every day, Lisa."

"How can you pray to a God who would let this happen to me?" Lisa slowly slurred the words, angry that her mother and sister were abandoning her.

"I don't know why this happened, but I do know that prayer works," Faith replied.

Lisa's anger turned to tears. "Please don't go."

If Lisa were honest with herself, she'd admit she was still in denial. As long as mother and sister were around, they created a diversion and she didn't have to deal with everything that had happened to her. When they left, she would be forced to face the hand she'd been dealt. She'd have to look in the mirror. The nurses had decided to cover the mirrors in her room, telling Faith it would be too traumatic for Lisa to see her appearance. Would Brian cover all the mirrors at home, too?

The following morning, after all her physicians signed off on her release papers, the trauma nurse who'd saved her life wheeled Lisa out of the hospital. Kelly helped her into the car while Brian placed her bag in the trunk. Kelly wished Lisa well and said her good-byes. She joined Brian at the rear of the car.

"Brian, it's going to be difficult for a while," she informed. "It's like starting over for her. She'll be irritable, unstable, and unpredictable."

He nodded.

"Just be patient with her. Give her time to heal mentally and emotionally, too."

The roller coaster ride was just beginning.

Chapter Six

Lisa was quiet during the ride home. She felt uncomfortable in the car; she was anxious. The doctor's had told her it might be frightening riding in the car. They also said she might not suffer any discomfort at all since she didn't remember anything from the day she was hit. Maybe she didn't remember, but she still felt uneasy.

She tensed when Brian swung into the condo parking lot. "I want to go back to the hospital," she slurred, panicked. "I'm not ready to come home."

"It's okay, Lisa," he soothed. "We'll just take it one day at a time."

He parked the car and raced around to her door to help her out. She was a mere eighty-nine pounds and he was sometimes afraid to touch her for fear she would break. She leaned into him and together they entered their home.

Once inside, she asked for his help. "I need to go to the bathroom."

He helped her to the bathroom and at the doorway she told him she could manage the rest of the way on her own. She painfully inched her way forward and almost collided with the sink. She would never get used to being blind in one eye. It often made her feel as though she were off balance.

"I'm going to get your suitcase out of the car," he said. "I'll check on you in a minute."

When he was gone, she noticed the mirror wasn't covered. Now was as good a time as any to view the extent of her injuries. She slowly moved to stand in front of the mirror, but kept her gaze down. She couldn't spend the rest of her life avoiding mirrors…it was now or never. Slowly, she lifted her head and looked at her reflection.

She gasped. The woman looking back at her was a complete stranger! She became lightheaded and leaned into the sink to steady herself. It wasn't her face; it was someone else's. It wasn't her nose, or her mouth. The shape of her face was no longer oval and her almond-shaped eyes were gone. Who was this person? The longer she looked, the angrier she became.

She reached for a tube of lipstick and scrawled the words *"I'm Ruined"* across the mirror. The tears turned to hysteria. She pounded her fists against the wall-mounted mirror trying to shatter it. She had no strength and couldn't even shatter it.

Brian heard the commotion from downstairs and he raced up the steps two at a time. Damn! He'd forgotten about the mirror. He burst through the bathroom door and grabbed her hands and pulled her into his embrace.

"I'm sorry, Lisa," he whispered. "I forgot to cover the mirror."

"I'm ugly!" she sobbed, pounding her fists on his chest until he released her. It was then he saw writing on the mirror. It was smudged, but he could still read it. He didn't know what to say. He didn't know what to do. There was no manual that had the answers.

The advice the nurses gave him came to his mind. *One day at a time…take it one day at a time.* He didn't want to take it one day at a time; he wanted things to be the way they were before.

"Lisa, let me fix you a cup of tea."

"I want to go to bed."

He helped her get situated in bed and fluffed the pillows for her to lean into. Because of her injuries, she was forced to sleep on her back all the time. She longed to be able to sleep on her side again. Once she was situated, he went to the kitchen and made her a cup of hot tea with lemon. He returned to her side and placed it on the bedside stand, then crawled into bed beside her. She drifted off to sleep and he would have too, but her moans and heavy breathing kept him awake.

The following weeks became routine. Brian bathed her every morning, cooked, cleaned, helped her get around or get situated in bed, and doled out her medicine; all he received in return was her disdain. She snapped at him for everything. Lisa wasn't used to being dependent on anyone and she hated it. She constantly complained about the pain with her eye and back. By nighttime, he fell into bed completely exhausted.

At one point, he'd hired a nurse to look after her while he was at work, but that didn't last long. Lisa hated the nurse and made the woman's job difficult. The nurse quit after only three days. He'd wanted to hire another, but Lisa said she would make her quit too. He gave up.

Their relationship deteriorated even more when he began drinking more than usual in the evenings. He'd come home, check on her, and pour himself a scotch. No matter how many times she lit into him—and pointed out it was a *drunk* driver who put her in this condition—he continued drinking.

He needed an escape—*fast*.

Emmit Pernell Hickson, attorney at law, sat behind his mahogany desk sizing up Brian Caulder who was seated opposite him. As Brian talked, Emmit frantically took notes on the yellow legal pad; he was already formulating the case in his mind as the facts were being shared with him.

Hickson, a traditional southern textbook lawyer, worshipped money. It was the main reason he went into law. He could tell the young man seated across from him worshipped it, too. Caulder had expensive tastes. He was well groomed, and he was wearing a trendy suit, an expensive watch, and designer shoes. In fact, he saw a bit of himself in his new client. He was able to size the man up immediately.

Brian had sized Emmit up, too, when he'd first walked into the attorney's office. He liked him immediately. Brian did his homework researching this lawyer that Angie had recommended and this one had an excellent track record. When he'd asked around about Hickson, consensus was it was hard to tell where the lawyer ended and the man began—a trait that many clients wanted in a lawyer—especially Brian.

"Was this Walter Fowler insured?"

"I sure hope so," Brian replied.

"I'll have my people check into it, just to make sure. Now, this nurse," Emmit paused to look at his tablet, "Kelly Brannigan. Do you think she would be willing to testify as to what she saw that morning?"

"I don't see why not," Brian replied.

"Well, we might be able to get Lisa one large settlement, and I think we might be able to get you one, too."

"I don't understand," Brian said.

"Not only can we file on Lisa's behalf, but you can file a loss of consortium suit," Emmit explained.

"What does that mean?"

"In the simplest terms, Mr. Caulder, it means that you can file suit because the accident prevented your wife from performing her, uh, wifely duties."

Brian refrained from smiling. He didn't want to appear too greedy. He couldn't believe he could collect money over the fact that he and Lisa hadn't had sex since the wreck. Had he known, it might have lessened his frustration over the past few months.

"How much money?"

"Well, don't hold me to this, but I reckon with everything you've told me, you're looking at about a hundred grand for your suit."

Brian's eyes widened. One hundred thousand dollars. He could find a lot of things to do with that kind of money. Like start over.

"Let's do it. I want to file a loss of consortium."

"First, you need to bring the little lady into my office to file her lawsuit; then we will file yours," Emmit directed.

After the meeting with the attorney, Brian returned to the condo. Lisa was seated on the sofa reading the newspaper.

"Where were you? You were gone a long time. What if I needed you?"

He ignored her. "I have to go out of town this weekend…on business. I've asked Sandra to come stay with you. She agreed."

Lisa was shocked, and angry. "You can't go away! I need you here with me."

He wasn't in the mood for her clinginess today. "I have to go. It's my job."

"Don't they know how serious my injuries are? How can they send you out of town when I need you to take care of me?"

"Don't forget, Lisa, it's my health insurance that's paying your medical bills," he said without emotion. "If I lose my job, you lose your health benefits. Is that what you want?"

She felt as though he'd punched her in the stomach. "No. I just don't want you to go."

She rose from the sofa and reached to hug him. He backed away. She moved in again and this time he closed his eyes and tolerated the gesture. When he tried to end the embrace, she clung even tighter.

"Lisa! Let go."

She backed away from him. "You don't love me anymore, do you?"

He was getting impatient. "Let me help you get into bed."

"I don't want to go to bed," she replied. "You think I'm ugly, don't you?"

When he didn't answer, she went on. "You don't have to say anything, I already know the answer."

"You're imaging things," he responded and went into the other room. He poured himself a drink and turned on the television. He didn't know how much more he could take. He was miserable. He was tired of taking care of her. She had become a burden. He was glad work was taking him out of town this week. He needed the break.

He heard her sobbing in the other room and he turned up the volume on the television to drown her out. He felt only a slight twinge of guilt.

The following morning, Lisa awoke to find Brian gone from the bed. She panicked. She was about to ease out of bed when the bedroom door open. He walked in carrying a tray that had her breakfast and a single red rose on it.

"Good morning, sleeping beauty," he greeted her.

"Thank you," she replied, grateful for the attention he was giving her.

Her mouth was still wired shut and eating hadn't gotten any easier. She struggled to eat the Cream of Wheat. At one point, she looked up to see that Brian was packing a suitcase.

"What are you doing," she asked in a panic.

"I told you, I have to go out of town today."

She slammed her spoon to the tray and cereal spattered on the satin sheets. "No, you didn't!"

"Yes, I did," he calmly replied. "You know you have problems with short-term memory, Lisa. I told you yesterday that I would be leaving. You forgot."

"I did not forget!" she countered.

Brian continued packing. "I'm not going to argue with you. Sandra will be here shortly. She'll stay with you while I'm gone."

Lisa threw her breakfast tray on the floor. Brian didn't move to pick it up. He finished packing instead. When he was done, he forced himself to lean down and kiss her on the forehead. "I'll see you when I get back."

He left the room.

The doorbell rang; it was Sandra.

"Man, am I glad to see you," he welcomed her with a hug.

"How is she?" Sandra asked, hugging him back.

"Not good. Thanks for coming, Sandra."

When he'd phoned her last week and asked her to fly down to Atlanta for a few days, she didn't know what to say. She was afraid to see Lisa. She didn't even have the guts to fly down when Lisa had been in the hospital. She'd spoken to her on the phone a couple of times since the crash, but this would be their first reunion since Lisa left Washington. She was nervous.

Brian showed Sandra around the condo—with the exception of his and Lisa's bedroom. He figured the two friends could get reacquainted after he left. He went over Lisa's medications with her, and showed her the list of important phone numbers, including everyone from Lisa's plastic surgeon to her physical therapist. They spoke for a few more minutes before Brian retrieved his suitcase and headed out the door. He was backing out of his parking space when he realized he'd forgotten about the mess Lisa had made in the bedroom. He rolled down the window and called to Sandra who was still standing at the door.

"Sandra, she left a mess on the bedroom floor. I'm sorry. I didn't have time to clean it up."

"I'll take care of it." She waved good-bye.

Sandra stood outside Lisa's bedroom wondering what kind of reception she would receive. Easing the door open, she saw someone who didn't even look like her friend sitting in the bed with tears streaming down her cheeks. Lisa was no longer the beautiful, carefree, confident woman she'd been when she left Washington. It broke Sandra's heart—until she spied the overturned tray on the floor and what she assumed was cream of wheat spattered on the carpet.

"Hey!" She waltzed into the room and greeted her friend as though everything was normal. "It's me!"

Lisa bypassed any greeting. "Where's Brian?"

"He just left."

"He didn't even say good-bye!" Lisa snapped.

Brian told Sandra that Lisa would often forget things that happened just moments before.

"Maybe you just forgot."

"I didn't forget," Lisa barked. "I would remember my husband saying good-bye to me."

Sandra didn't know what to say.

Lisa began crying. "He doesn't love me anymore. I don't blame him. Look at me!"

Sandra still didn't know what to say. After several uncomfortable minutes, Sandra checked Lisa's medication schedule and saw it was time for her pain medicine. She gave her two blue pills and a glass of water.

"You rest and I'll check back in on you when I'm done unpacking."

Lisa nodded and took the pills as she was instructed. She tried to get comfortable in bed, but no matter what position she shifted to, she was in pain.

The next few days were hard for Sandra. She had a new respect for what Brian had been going through. She'd only been there a few days and already she wanted to leave her friend. Lisa was anything but accommodating. She was argumentative, critical, and uncooperative. Her behavior was irrational on a good day and volatile on a bad day. All that she ever talked about were her injuries. She was drowning in a pool of self-pity.

Sandra helped Lisa get situated at the breakfast table one morning then brewed some coffee. Strong coffee. The aroma itself was enough to wake Sandra. She left the bacon on the stove burner too long and it burned. The smoke and stench worked its way throughout the downstairs rooms. She quickly switched the stove vent on hoping it would pull the smoke outside—fast! She didn't think she could take another lecture from Lisa about how she was doing everything wrong.

When the food was done, she placed it on the table. "Lisa, I'm sorry about the burnt-bacon smell. I turned on the vent, it should clear out in a few minutes."

Lisa replied in a monotone voice, "Didn't Brian tell you? I can't smell anything, any more."

"I'm sorry."

Sandra opened the window blinds in the dining room and Lisa snapped at her. "Shut those. The light bothers my eye."

Sandra closed the blinds.

Lisa tried to eat her Cream of Wheat, but she couldn't. She shoved the bowl away from her. "I can't eat this. It's too thick."

Sandra took the bowl. "I'll add more water." She threw the hot cereal into the blender and added hot water to thin it. It was now liquefied.

Lisa tried again and still struggled to get the Cream of Wheat down. "I don't want any more. It's too difficult to eat it."

Sandra looked at Lisa and didn't know her anymore. There were no traces of the young, confident woman who'd left a high-profile career in Washington, D.C. just over a year ago. Tears glazed her eyes and she ate the rest of her bacon and eggs in silence, not knowing what else to do.

Later that morning, Sandra washed Lisa's hair—a task that was difficult due to the two wire antennas still protruding from her head. When she was done, she saw a spark of her old friend.

"Thank you, Sandra," Lisa said in a soft tone. "That's the longest I've gone without thinking about the pain. Can you please get me my pain medication?"

Sandra was near exhaustion by the time Brian returned from his trip. Lisa was in bed when she'd heard the front door open, then heard Brian's voice. Thank God he was home! He could take care of her now.

A few weeks later, although she was still having difficulty remembering things, and thinking clearly, Lisa wanted to return to work. She approached Brian after he'd returned from work one evening. She caught him as soon as he walked in the door — before he reached for the bottle of scotch.

"Brian, I want to go back to work."

"We can talk about that later, Lisa," he changed the subject. "What did you do today?"

"Can we talk about it now?"

Uh-oh. She wasn't going to give up, he thought. "Lisa, I have something to tell you. You better sit down." He led her to the sofa.

"What is it?"

Brian knew there was no easy way to tell her, so he just blurted it out. "They gave Vanessa your job."

"They did what!" she screamed. "Vanessa got my job?"

Brian rubbed her back and spoke soothingly. "Lisa, you aren't ready to go back to work yet."

She started crying. "It isn't fair! They didn't hold my job for me!"

Brian was used to her sobbing and put his arm around her. She leaned into him and cried until she couldn't cry any longer.

When Lisa was finally able to leave the condo and venture outside, she didn't. The thought of people seeing her face, was too much. She was used to people staring at her — but that was out admiration. She didn't want anyone staring at her bruises and swollen face, not to mention her lopsided eye.

Her traffic court date was quickly approaching and she knew she had to attend. She felt very insecure and needed Brian to go with her. She was relieved when he agreed to go.

She fantasized about putting the drunk driver who destroyed her life behind bars. She wanted to ruin his life like he'd ruined hers. She also wanted to keep him off the roads so the he could never hurt anyone else.

On the morning of the hearing, Lisa spent a long time in the bathroom applying makeup. No matter how much she applied, she still thought she looked hideous. How could she ever show her face in public? She was ugly! She just knew that people would gawk and point at her.

Brian finally coaxed her from the bathroom and they headed out the door. She was walking better now, but still with a noticeable limp from her fractured pelvic bone that was not yet completely healed.

In the courtroom, while waiting for their case to be heard, Lisa felt all eyes on her. She willed herself to remain in the room, even though she wanted to run. Seated behind her were Kelly Brannigan, the trauma nurse who freed her from the wreckage and treated her on the scene; the truck driver who'd witnessed the crash and pulled his rig over to help her; and four other witnesses from the scene. Walter Fowler, the drunk driver, was seated adjacent to her, which made her feel extremely uncomfortable. He didn't even look at her. He stared straight ahead and even appeared indignant.

One by one, the witnesses, and Lisa, took the stand and gave their compelling testimony. It was strange for Lisa to hear these strangers talk about events that happened to her that she didn't even remember. The fact that she didn't remember was probably a good thing. If she had, she would probably never get into a car again—ever!

When the judge heard all the testimonies, he was ready to hand down the verdict.

"I find the defendant Walter Fowler guilty on all charges."

Lisa let out a breath of relief.

"Mr. Fowler," the judge continued. "You are hereby fined four-hundred and fifty dollars."

Lisa gasped. Others in the courtroom did, too. How could the sentence be so light? Dammit! This man stole her life from her and he received a four-hundred-fifty-dollar fine? What was wrong with the judge?

She stood up. "Four hundred and fifty dollars?" she said loud enough for everyone in the courtroom to hear. "He took my life away from me and all he gets is a lousy fine?"

The judge called for order in the courtroom. Brian quickly ushered Lisa outside. He was walking too fast and in trying to keep up with him, she accidentally bumped into someone on her left side.

"Hey, watch where you're going, lady!"

Lisa grabbed the sleeve of Brian's shirt. She couldn't trust her eyesight to maneuver her through the crowded hallway.

He gently took her hand as they walked out of the courthouse. Once outside, she spotted Kelly Brannigan and took the opportunity to thank her.

Lisa kept reliving the hearing in her mind during the drive home. When they'd finally reached the condo, she finally spoke.

"He didn't even apologize," she whispered. "He took my life away and didn't even say he was sorry. He didn't even look at me!"

"What did you expect from a drunk driver?" Brian replied.

"I wanted an apology!"

"Well, you didn't get one so get over it."

Tears filled her eyes. She wanted Brian to say something kind to her…to love her…to protect her…to help her forget the pain.

She tried to hug him and he moved away from her. Had he done that on purpose? She tried again to move into his embrace. He turned to the wet bar and poured a scotch.

"Brian," she began, not sure if he was moving away on purpose. "I want you to hold me."

Instead of accommodating her, he left the room.

Lisa was stunned. She eased into the lounge chair and spent the remainder of the afternoon paging through their photo albums. She cried when she leafed through the one that had their honeymoon pictures. She found one of her where she was in her skimpy bathing suit. She was beautiful in the picture and the past few months seemed like a dream. Where was the beautiful woman in the picture? Why had God taken from her the one gift that everyone admired in her?

She crumpled the picture in her fist and threw it across the room. It wasn't fair...it just wasn't fair. She sobbed until she fell asleep in the chair.

It was after midnight when Brian entered the living room to find her sleeping. He'd had about four stiff scotches and was feeling pretty good. He flipped the television on and turned to an adult channel. After watching for a while, he became aroused. He shook Lisa and told her it was time to come to bed.

She turned down the covers and crawled into bed. He crawled into bed beside her and began massaging her back. He didn't stop there. He passionately kissed her face that was hidden in the shadows. During the kiss, she moved slightly out of the shadows and into the moonlight. It was then he got a glimpse of her face and felt as though a bucket of ice water had been thrown on him. He turned from her and muttered, "Damn it!"

"What's wrong, Brian?"

"What isn't?" he returned in a sarcastic tone.

"Did I do something wrong?"

"Yea. You got in that stupid wreck."

Lisa was suddenly very aware of her altered appearance. She turned away from him. "I can't help the way I look."

"I know you can't," he agreed. "But you have to look at it from my point of view."

He left the room and she wondered where he'd gone. In a few minutes he returned. He smoothed the photo Lisa had crumpled just hours before. He looked at it with longing in his eyes before turning it for her to see.

"This is my point of view," he told her, the words half-slurred. "I married a beautiful, sexy woman and now look at you." He gestured toward her frail, thin body.

"Please don't say that, Brian," she begged him.

He sank to the edge of the bed. She eased herself to the floor at his feet and clung to him. "I love you, Brian. I need you. Please don't turn away from me now. You're all I have left."

"I always said I would have the best of everything."

"Don't Brian," she pleaded.

"Why not? Let's get it all out in the open right now."

"You're drunk!"

"You bet I am. Wanna' join me?"

"Dr. Howden said I shouldn't drink while I'm taking my medicine."

"Dr. Howden and I spoke this week. He thinks he can fix your face. Not like you looked before, but at least better than the way you look now."

She couldn't believe he was being so cruel. It intensified her shame. But it also gave her courage.

"Look, I'm sorry if sex doesn't come in the same pretty package you're used to, but I'm still a woman and *I'm still your wife!*"

Brian gulped the rest of his drink and left the room. He was glad he'd provoked the fight. Now he could leave without feeling guilty. He got into his car and drove to the nearest pay phone. He pulled the worn business card from his wallet and dialed the number on the back of the card.

Chapter Seven

Brian pulled his car into the parking lot of a bar across town. He parked around the rear of the building so that his vehicle couldn't be seen from the main road. He entered the bar and was thankful it was smoke-filled, less chance of anyone recognizing him through the haze. He searched the crowd for familiar faces and he found none. Good.

He took a seat at the bar and eyed the sexy bartender. When she spotted him, he winked.

"What's your pleasure, cowboy?" she asked in a sexy tone.

He ran his fingers through his thick black hair. "Scotch on the rocks."

She placed the drink on the bar and he downed it in one gulp. "Another one."

"You look like you might have had a few before you came here."

He didn't respond. Instead he turned his gaze to two blondes sitting at a nearby table. When he tired of looking at them, he watched some babes on the dance floor. Drink in hand, he staggered in the direction of the dance floor. Before he could make it, he bumped into a tall, slender woman and spilled his drink down the front of him.

"Damn!"

"That's what you get for stepping out on your wife," the soft voice seductively purred. "It took you long enough to call."

Brian took the napkin that Vanessa offered. She looked hotter than ever.

"I've been busy," he slurred.

Vanessa felt somewhat slighted that he called during a drinking binge, and not when he was sober. Somehow, the conquest didn't seem as monumental now.

She led him to an empty table. When they were seated, she lit a cigarette. "So, are you going to buy me a drink?"

Brian's head was still in a fog. "A drink. Sure." He flagged their waitress and gave their drink orders.

"So, why aren't you with Lisa tonight?"

"I needed a break."

Vanessa wondered what his idea of a "break" was. She took a puff on her cigarette and glanced around the bar.

"It's awful noisy and crowded here," she said, snuffing out the cigarette in the ashtray "Why don't we go to my place? I've got a bottle of thirty-year-old sour mash begging to be opened."

Brian knew he was drunk and he didn't care. He felt free. For weeks he'd taken care of Lisa and he was tired of it. Tonight, he would have fun. Hadn't he earned it after all?

"Sure," he slurred. "Let's go to your place, Vanessa."

He pulled his wallet from of his pocket and after trying numerous times to remove a twenty-dollar bill from the folds, he gave up and tossed the wallet on the table.

"What are you doing?" she asked.

He threw his head back and laughed. "Hell, she can just keep the wallet!"

Vanessa rolled her eyes and removed a twenty from the wallet. They stood up from the table and she took the opportunity to slip the wallet back into his rear pocket.

She helped him to her car. The ride to her apartment was sobering for Brian. The radio was playing and the windows were open. The crisp night air helped clear his head.

When they arrived, he looked around Vanessa's apartment and noted she had expensive taste. He liked that. He plopped down on the sofa while she brought out the bottle of sour mash. She poured them each a glass and sat on the sofa beside him.

He took a sip and savored the taste. "That's good stuff, Vanessa."

She smiled devilishly. "Mmm. It is, isn't it?"

"I like it."

She placed her drink on the coffee table and took Brian by surprise when planted a kiss on his lips.

Brian moaned and deepened the kiss. "Which way to the bedroom?" he asked, his heart pounding in his chest.

Vanessa pointed down the hall and he easily lifted her and carried her to the bedroom.

The following morning Vanessa dropped Brian off at his car and the two stopped at a small coffee shop for breakfast. They were no sooner seated in their booth that Vanessa lit up a cigarette. The fact that Vanessa was a chain smoker was one thing Brian didn't like about her.

"Last night was wonderful, Brian," she told him, staring into his eyes.

He smiled. "Then I guess we'll have to make this a regular thing."

Vanessa got serious for a moment. "What about Lisa?"

"Let's not talk about her, okay?"

"Sure." Vanessa's gaze moved past him to a couple that was eying them from the doorway of the coffee shop. She recognized the couple, but she didn't remember from where.

Angie's mouth dropped when she spied Brian and Vanessa sitting at a booth inside the coffee shop. She took a couple of steps in their direction and Stuart took a hold of her.

"Angie, what are you doing? It's none of our business!"

"I'm going to give them both a piece of my mind!" she seethed. "Of all the people! Why would he choose someone who hated Lisa as much as Vanessa did?"

"Not here, Angie."

Brian noticed Vanessa was distracted. "You haven't been listening to me for the past five minutes, Vanessa. Where are you?"

"Brian, do you know that couple standing at the take-out window?"

Brian turned. "Damn!" It was Stuart and Angie and they were staring directly at him and Vanessa.

"Come on. Let's go." He threw a ten on the table.

"Stuart, Angie!" Brian greeted when he reached the couple. "What are you two doing here?"

Angie glowered at him. "We're getting coffee. What are you two doing here?"

"I stopped by for some coffee, too, and saw Vanessa having breakfast. So I joined her," he delivered the lie then turned to Vanessa. "Thanks for the company, Vanessa. You have a good day." He held the door open for her and fortunately, he was the only one who could see that she rolled her eyes at him. She walked across the parking lot and got into her car.

"Well, it was good seeing you both," Brian said and exited the coffee shop.

"Stuart! Do something!" Angie ordered.

Stuart placed a five-dollar bill in Angie's hand to pay for their order and he dashed out the door. He reached Brian's car as he was about to drive off. He banged on the hood.

"Stuart! What the hell are you doing?" Brian yelled out the window.

"What the hell am I doing? What the hell are *you* doing?"

Brian played dumb. "What are you talking about?"

"Vanessa made Lisa's life Hell every day the two of them worked together. Why are you all of a sudden chummy-chummy with her?"

"We're not chummy-chummy. I told you I was getting some coffee and ran into her."

"Knock it off, Brian." Stuart shook his head. "Don't try to con me. You forget, I cheated on my wife for years."

"Then what are you doing chastising me, you self-righteous son of a bitch," Brian shouted as he got out of his car.

"For the record, I stopped cheating months ago. It's not worth it," Stuart replied. He realized how loud they had been arguing and he lowered his voice. "Does Lisa know?"

Brian finally realized he couldn't lie his way out of this one. "No, of course not. I'm not that cruel."

Stuart didn't know what to say.

Brian looked off into the distance. "I tried to make love to Lisa last night. It would have been the first time since that bastard hit her." He leaned against the car. "I needed four drinks before I could even muster up the courage to touch her. And then, when I saw her face, I knew I couldn't. She looked awful."

"Grow up, Brian," Stuart reproved. "You're doing your thinking from below your belt."

"You don't know what it's like, Stuart. You can't possibly understand."

Brian got back into his car.

"You may be right, Brian," Stuart called. "But did it have to be Vanessa?"

Brian started the engine and sped off.

Lisa was up early that morning and had the coffee brewing when Brian finally walked in the door. He looked awful; his hair was a mess and his clothes were wrinkled. On the front of his shirt was a large stain. When he walked by her, she immediately smelled the liquor.

"Where were you last night?" she asked.

"I needed to think. I drove around all night."

"Since when do you keep a bottle of scotch in your car?" she pushed.

"What are you talking about?"

"You smell like liquor and cigarettes. Did you take up smoking last night, too?"

How could he have been so stupid? He should have changed into the spare shirt he kept in the trunk for emergencies. He was busted.

"I stopped at a bar for a drink."

"You were pretty well lit when you left last night," her eyes widened. "Don't you remember it was a drunk driver who did this to me?"

"Lisa, look," he started. "I'm sorry about last night. Okay? You've suffered a great deal; I know that. But I've suffered too. I'm going through a lot, too." He ran his hand through his hair.

"Look, let's just forget about last night, okay?"

She let her guard down and hugged him. "I was so worried about you last night. Please don't leave me like that again."

"I won't. I promise."

After a few moments, he pulled away from her embrace. "I'm going to shower."

"Wait," she called after him. "I have some good news to tell you."

With all the bad things that had happened, it was about time he heard some good news. He turned to look at her, but when he did, guilt shot through him. He averted his gaze from hers. "What's the good news?"

"The attorney, Emmit Hickson, called about the lawsuit. He wants to meet with both of us."

She had his attention.

"Fowler was working for Kinderland Auto Sales."

"We already knew that," he replied.

"But what we didn't know was that Fowler was on company time when he hit me. He was on his way to show a client the car he was driving."

Brian smiled for the first time that morning. "That means we can sue the dealership."

"Yes!" Lisa was glad he was smiling. She hadn't seen him smile in a long time. "We'll be able to get enough money to pay off the medical bills."

He hugged her and kissed her cheek. "Hey, babe, have you had breakfast yet?"

"No, just coffee."

He kissed the tip of her awkward-looking nose. "Why don't I go out and get us some breakfast?" Before she could respond, he was out the door.

He hopped back inside his car and headed to the phone booth down the road. He pulled some coins from his pocket and placed a call.

"Emmit Hickson, please," he said to the secretary.

After a few moments, the attorney picked up on the line. "Emmit Hickson."

"Emmit, this is Brian Caulder."

"Brian, hello. Did Lisa give you the good news?"

"Yes, she did. But I just wanted to check and make sure that I could still file the loss of consortium."

"Yes, you can, and we may be able to get you even more of a settlement in light of the recent findings."

"Just don't let Lisa know that we talked about the loss of consortium suit." Brian was glad he was still going to get a settlement because he felt he earned it.

Lisa crossed her thin legs and folded her hands on her lap while Emmit reread her file. Brian sat next to her and reached over and gently placed his hand on her thigh to stop her from nervously tapping her foot. She stopped tapping that one, but started tapping the other.

Emmit finally spoke. "Mrs. Caulder," he leaned back into his chair and took another bite of his hamburger and didn't hesitate to talk with his mouth full. "This guy Fowler hasn't got any money, as you both know. But I had a private eye check into the finances of Kinderland and it seems they're not doing too bad. In fact, financially, they're sitting pretty."

"We're not looking to get rich from my injuries," Lisa interjected. "We just want money to pay off the medical bills. We still owe a great deal."

"Lisa," Brian stopped her. "If Mr. Hickson feels he can get us a sizeable settlement, I say we go for it. You don't know what tomorrow holds. You may never be able to go back to work. If we ask for only enough to pay off the medical bills, we'll be right back where we started from."

Brian had a point.

"Don't forget, Mrs. Caulder," Emmit added his two cents. "I get one-third of whatever the court awards you, forty-percent if there's an appeal."

Lisa didn't like Emmit Hickson from that point on. He was only representing her for the money, not because he felt she'd been wronged.

After they left his office, he asked his secretary to come into his office. This was the third secretary he'd gone through in only a year. He was a difficult boss to say the least.

When the secretary didn't move as fast as he would have liked, he shouted into the outer office, "Judy! I said come in here!"

Judy picked up her steno pad and pencil and hurried into Emmit's office. Lisa wasn't the only one who didn't like him, his secretary obviously had problems with him as well.

"Let's get to work on the Caulder case," he said.

On Friday morning, Brian and Lisa sat at the dining room table eating breakfast. Although they were beside each other, they were worlds apart. Brian was eating a healthy portion of bacon and eggs while Lisa was trying to suck oatmeal through her wired mouth.

"People sure do take eating for granted," she said, hoping to get his attention.

He nodded, pretending to pay attention, and took another bite of his bagel.

Lisa eyed her oatmeal, then the bagel. She wondered what the bagel would taste like pureed in the blender. She wrinkled her nose at the thought of what it would look like. She'd stick to her oatmeal.

Of Face Value

By the time she inhaled the last of the oatmeal through her wired mouth, Brian had long been gone from the table. She could hear him upstairs packing. He was heading to Jacksonville on a business trip. She cleared the table and joined him in the bedroom.

"I wish you didn't have to leave," she sighed.

He was glad he would be getting away for a few days, but he kept it to himself. "Angie will be here to take care of you. You two will have fun. And tomorrow you get your mouth unwired. The days will fly by and before you know it, I'll be back."

Lisa wrapped her arms around him and whispered, "I love you."

Brian backed away from her and gave her a quick peck on the cheek. "Me too, babe. I have to get going now if I'm going to catch my plane." He picked up his luggage and headed down the hall. "See you in a few days."

The following morning, Angie took Lisa to the hospital for her outpatient surgery to remove the wires from her jaw. Lisa was feeling jittery; hospitals now made her feel that way. Dr. Howden reassured her that it was a minor procedure and she would be fine. She couldn't help but feel that Dr. Howden showed her more compassion than her husband. As the physician guided her down the hallway, she turned to Angie who was seated in the waiting area leafing through a fashion magazine.

Brian's business meeting finished early that morning. He grabbed a cup of coffee and a quick bite to eat before heading back to his room at the Jacksonville Hilton. He set his coffee down, picked up the phone, and dialed.

83

A voice on the other end answered in a seductive voice. "Hello?"

"The meeting let out early. I'm in my room."

"I'll be right there," she purred.

Dr. Howden slowly removed Lisa's wires one-by-one. When he was finished, Lisa was wheeled to the recovery room. It took a few hours for the anesthesia to wear off. She patiently waited for Dr. Howden to come in and speak with her. She liked him. He was a very kind, gentle man who had her best interest at heart and she appreciated that about him. If only Brian displayed those same qualities.

The doctor finally entered the room and smiled at her. "How does it feel?"

Her jaw was stiff and she couldn't move it. She thought that once the wires were out she'd be free. She still couldn't open her mouth! She was disappointed and he saw it in her eyes.

"It will take time for your mouth to open," he cautioned. "Even when it does, you'll still only be able to eat soft foods. When you are able to open your mouth fully, then we'll talk about braces."

She nodded. She wanted to smile, but couldn't. She was too disappointed.

"I told Angie that you'll be ready to leave in about a half hour," he informed and added, "You're doing fine, Lisa. Remember, just one day at a time."

Angie helped Lisa into the passenger's side of the car and the two girls drove back to the condo in silence. Angie knew not to ask too many questions of Lisa. She'd come to learn that Lisa would share what she wanted to share in her own time. Angie would never pressure her.

When they were settled in the condo, Lisa began to cry. Angie rushed over to hug her.

"Brian and I planned a dinner party tomorrow evening to celebrate having the wires removed and being able to eat like everyone else," Lisa told her. "And I still can't open my mouth more than a half inch."

Angie rubbed Lisa's back. "Give it time," she whispered to her friend.

"I should call Brian to let him know that we won't be celebrating," Lisa said, then dialed the number to Brian's hotel in Jacksonville. "Room 412, please," she said into the mouthpiece.

She let the phone ring ten times before hanging up the phone. She wondered where he could be. His meeting was supposed to be over by now and he said he'd wait for her call.

Vanessa was sprawled across the bed puffing on a cigarette. Brian lay next to her wearing nothing but a grin on his face.

"You sure know how to please a man," he said, feeling very relaxed.

Vanessa took another hit of her cigarette. "What I want to know is how you got Lisa to believe your business meeting was going to last three days?" Did she lose her brain in that accident, too?"

Brian's facial features turned serious and he sat up. "There was brain damage."

Vanessa didn't feel bad for mocking Lisa. In reality, Lisa's hardship led to Vanessa's promotion. How could she feel bad?

She snuffed her cigarette in the ashtray. "Do you love her?"

Brian thought for a moment. "I will always love the Lisa I fell in love with; the Lisa I married. But I lost her in the wreck. She died." He began rubbing Vanessa's back. "But I don't love who she is now. I don't even know the person she is now."

He gave Vanessa a playful swat on her rear. "Let's not talk about her anymore. We have the whole afternoon to ourselves."

Vanessa swung her legs over the side of the bed and started getting dressed.

"What are you doing?" he asked.

"I'm going back to Atlanta."

"But we have the entire afternoon. Why are you leaving now? What's wrong?"

Vanessa thought for a moment, as though she were trying to find the perfect words to respond to him.

"Let's just say your revelations took the fun out of the affair."

He was confused. "What are you talking about?"

"Well, Brian," she cooed, "it's like this. I wanted Lisa's job and I got it. The only sad part was that I couldn't be the one to tell her. The expression on her face hearing it come from me would have been priceless."

"I don't under—"

"Second of all," she cut him off. She was now dressed and placing her clothes in her suitcase. "I wanted you."

"But you have me," he replied.

"Yes," she agreed. "But the whole idea behind getting you was to be able to flaunt it in her face. And with your little revelation that she suffered brain damage, well. it just wouldn't have the same impact. I guess it's a little like you said: I hated the Lisa I knew before the accident; I wanted to hurt the Lisa who worked at Bartonelli's East. But that person doesn't exist now, does she? She died in the accident."

"You cold bitch," Brian snorted. His angry expression slowly subsided and he smiled. "That's what turns me on. How about one for the road?"

Vanessa picked up her suitcase. "Goodbye, Brian." She opened the door and stepped through. Before closing it, she turned to offer him one final sentiment. "By the way, you weren't that great. I've slept with hotel bellboys who are more experienced than you." With that, she slammed the door.

Although her last comment bruised his ego, all he could do was laugh…hysterically. What more could go wrong in his life?

Chapter Eight

Before Brian could even use his key to unlock the front door, it burst open and Angie stepped outside and closed the door. The scowl on her face told him he was in for a scolding.

"Where have you been? You were supposed to be here hours ago," Angie vented. "I called the airport and know what time your flight arrived, so don't give me some crap about it being late."

"I stopped for a drink at the airport lounge. Is that now a crime?" He tried to open the door but she blocked his path.

"Lisa's not doing well. She's been patiently waiting for you to come home."

Where've you been, Angie, Brian thought to himself. Lisa's never doing well. If Angie had to put up with the things he'd had to put up for the past few months, she'd want to spend as much time away from the condo, too.

Only when Brian wiped the irresponsible smile from his face did she move away from the door to let him pass.

As he entered the condo, he called out, "Where is she? All she needs is a little of that Caulder magic."

He spied her lounging on the sofa and greeted her with a hug and kiss on the cheek. "I'm sorry I couldn't be at the hospital, Lisa," he apologized. "What happened?"

Tears were streaming down her cheeks. "I can only open my mouth a half inch. I had to cancel our dinner party for tomorrow night."

He put his arms around her. "We'll just do it another night, babe." He turned to Angie. "Thanks for being here for Lisa. I can take it from here."

Angie placed her hand on Lisa's shoulder. "Call me if you need anything. Promise?"

Lisa nodded. "I will. Thanks for everything, Angie."

When Angie was gone, Brian headed to the wet bar and poured himself a scotch. Lisa was disappointed, but didn't want to start an argument.

"Brian, Mr. Hickson called while you were out of town."

She had his attention immediately. "What did he say?"

"The car dealership that Mr. Fowler worked for has a sizeable insurance policy. He's confident that we're going to get more than enough to pay the bills."

Brian contained his excitement. That meant he would probably get a bigger settlement, too, in his loss of consortium suit.

"That's nice, Lisa. But even if we don't get a large settlement, we'll manage somehow."

Lisa smiled. "You are so good to me."

He downed his scotch.

"Oh, I almost forgot my other good news," she said. "I spoke with Dr. Howden and he's ready to schedule more plastic surgery. I can't wait. I'm tired of being ugly."

Brian placated her. "I told you, Lisa, that doesn't matter to me anymore. Sure, I had problems adjusting at first; who wouldn't have? But I realize now that I am in love with what really makes you Lisa. If I have to spend the rest of my life making you see that, well, that's just what I'll have to do."

Lisa was touched by his kind words and smiled. "I'm so glad you're home. I missed you so much."

"I missed you, too," he replied. "Let me get you your pain medication and we'll go to bed."

"All right."

After she took the pain pills, Brian took her hand and led her up the steps to the bedroom.

Lisa tossed and turned for most of the night. At one point, she bolted upright and screamed from a bad dream. She was drenched in sweat and reached across for Brian to hold her. He was gone!

"Brian!" she called out. "Brian, where are you?" He was gone and she was frightened and alone.

Brian sat at the bar downing his fourth scotch, eyeing all the cuties in the room. A slender, blonde gave him a sexy smile. He grinned from ear-to-ear and motioned the girl to join him. She gyrated across the dance floor in his direction and when she reached him, she folded into his arms. They danced, thigh-to-thigh, and he could tell she was on the make. He whispered something in her ear and she smiled. They left the bar and went back to her apartment.

The day of Lisa's plastic surgery at Northridge came quickly and before she knew it, it was time to remove the bandages. She sat facing Dr. Howden and the fact that her foot was tapping rapidly on the floor let him know she was very nervous.

She reached out for Brian. "Honey, please come hold my hand while he takes the bandages off."

Lisa didn't see Brian roll his eyes at her request, but the nurse did. She felt sorry for the young girl.

Brian plastered a smile on his face and moved beside her. He took her hand in his. "Right here, babe."

Dr. Howden slowly peeled away the bandages. As he worked, he cautioned her, "Lisa, I have to tell you that even though the operation was a measured success, this was only a most preliminary type operation."

Lisa froze as the last bandage was peeled away. She looked at Dr. Howden's face to see any type of emotion that might let her know how she looked. She couldn't read him.

He used a small flashlight to examine her face and said to the nurse, "See here, there's more facial structure and her cheek bones are more defined." Nonetheless, he finally nodded his approval.

Brian, however, didn't see any marked difference. He had been hoping for a miracle.

Dr. Howden handed Lisa a mirror, but before she looked he warned her, "There is still a lot of bruising from the operation."

Lisa slowly raised the mirror. She inventoried a face that she still didn't consider hers and it was still ugly. She slammed the mirror to the floor, shattering it into a million pieces.

"I'm still ugly!" she cried, startling everyone in the room—even Brian. But as far as he was concerned, she was right.

Dr. Howden had tried to prepare Lisa. He knew that anything less than looking like her old self was unacceptable.

She buried her face in her hands and continued to cry. What started out as sobbing turned into hysteria and she began hyperventilating. The nurse quickly gave her an oxygen mask.

Brian made no move to console her, which infuriated Dr. Howden. Didn't her husband realize she needed his support now more than she ever did?

Dr. Howden reached over and touched Lisa's shoulder. "We'll let the two of you alone. The nurse will be outside if you need anything."

When she had finally caught her breath, she put the mask down and buried her face in Brian's chest. He stroked her back, but it was more mechanical than compassionate. He just stood staring at the wall. His expression lacked any emotion.

Days turned into weeks and Lisa's mood grew lighter and lighter as the swelling went down in her face. The bruises were gone and she was able to open her mouth a little more. Even so, she was still only able to eat soft foods: mashed potatoes and applesauce. Of course, there was always soup, but she was quickly approaching the point where she loathed soup.

She began to view each day as a challenge—mentally, physically, and emotionally. She was making great strides, but still had a long way to go.

Brian's mood grew darker with each passing day. At times, she would catch him staring at her with the oddest expression on his face that she found hard to read. Maybe his foul mood didn't even have anything to do with her, she would tell herself. Maybe things at his office were bad. It couldn't be her. She wasn't as ugly as she was before this last round of surgery. Still, it had been weeks since he'd touched her. She couldn't even remember the last time he held her—*really held her*, not just placated her.

Lisa was seated at the table trying to eat a bowl of applesauce when Brian entered the kitchen. She had a mirror situated in front of her so she could watch the movements of her mouth and coordinate them with the movements of her hand. She couldn't help thinking the straw had been easier.

"This is hard!"

"I can imagine," Brian replied, but refused to look at her. He never looked at her. "I have to leave. I have to be at a meeting in fifteen minutes."

With that, he leaned down and gave her a small peck on the forehead and headed out the door.

She couldn't help seeing the irony in her situation. Each day, she became stronger and stronger; yet each day, their relationship faded just a little more.

Christmas came quickly and Lisa was surprised by the beautiful diamond necklace that Brian gave her. It was exquisite and she couldn't wait to wear it. She was excited by the gift because to her, it meant he still loved her.

Brian made plans to take her out for a New Year's celebration. She was thrilled to be getting out for an evening. That afternoon, she tried on every dress in her closet and nothing fit. One by one the articles of clothing were removed from the hanger, tried on, then removed, and tossed onto the floor in a heap. Finally, there was nothing left hanging in her closet. She was just about to give up when she remembered her red velvet dress. She opened the wardrobe and pulled it out. After removing the plastic garment bag, she pulled the dress over her head and she didn't even have to wiggle into it; it slid right down her thin, frail body. She edged to the mirror, almost afraid to look. When she finally did, tears filled her eyes.

The dress hung on her and did not appear the least bit flattering. She couldn't help remembering how she once filled the dress with her shapely figure. She quickly tore off the dress she once adored and flung it to the heap already on the floor.

"I'm not going out!" she cried. "Nothing fits any more!"

Brian wasn't in the mood for one of her emotional outbursts and shouted back, "Fine, you probably got in that wreck just to get attention." He stormed out of the condo.

Lisa was devastated by his remark and sobbed uncontrollably. Later, she pulled out the photo album of her Washington days. She sat on the bed and looked at the pictures taken at the Sheraton Park Hotel. She smiled when she got to the picture of her in her red velvet dress. She had been beautiful and shapely. She continued flipping the pages and came to the picture of her with the Nixons. She felt a wave of nostalgia pass over her. She missed her old life more than she ever dreamed she would. She never before realized how monumental her sacrifices had been for Brian, for their "perfect" life that didn't turn out so perfect.

She tossed the photo album on the floor and began pounding her fists into the pillow. "Why me?" she cried. "Why did this have to happen to me?"

Brian came home later that night and slept in the guestroom. They barely spoke to one another that weekend. She was thankful when Monday finally arrived and he went to work. She was just about to clean the kitchen when the phone ran. It was Emmit Hickson.

"Mornin' Lisa. How are you feeling?"

Lisa wasn't in the mood to exchange pleasantries with him. "I've felt better."

"Listen, we've hit a little snag with your case—but that's not unusual," he snickered. "That's the way it is with the legal system."

"What are you talking about? Is there a problem?"

"Well, the folks over at Kinderland Auto said that this Fowler guy wasn't working for them at the time of the collision."

The news was disheartening to her.

"What exactly does that mean, Mr. Hickson?"

"It's just a delaying tactic on their part. I don't really think there's a problem here. They're just searching for loopholes."

"How long until we go to trial?" she hesitated to ask.

"I can't give you a time, Lisa. Just be patient."

Easier said than done, she thought. The sooner her and Brian's dealings with Emmit Hickson were concluded, the better she would feel. He made her skin crawl at times, even though she couldn't quite put her finger on why.

"Oh, Lisa, I almost forgot to tell you—"

"Tell me what?"

"I've made arrangements for you to start attending a therapy clinic operated by Northridge Hospital."

Lisa was confused. Why was he involving himself in her rehabilitation? "I already see a therapist, Mr. Hickson."

"Yes, I understand," he placated her. "I talked to your therapist and we both agreed that this would be good for you. The sessions at Northridge are called group therapy. It's designed to help people adjust to a new life…you know, reclaim control of their lives. I've heard they do a good job."

"Are you saying that I need mental help?"

"You know that's not what I'm saying. You just need someone to talk to, that's all."

"I have Brian," she replied. "I don't need anyone else."

"Well they've opened up a space for you," he continued, as though he didn't hear her refusal, "and want you to start right away. They're expecting you tomorrow."

"But—"

"Good. I knew you'd understand. Oh, and be sure to begin keeping a diary. Also make a note of things you used to be able to do, but can't do any longer. Listen, I gotta' run across town. We'll talk later. You take care now."

"But—"

He hung up. Her mind filled with paranoid thoughts. Why did he think she needed mental counseling? Had Brian said something to Hickson? Her mind filled with frightening thoughts...straight jackets...mental wards...insanity. Her fear took over and she began to cry.

Chapter Nine

Angie dropped Lisa off at the Northridge Hospital Day Treatment program. Lisa's stomach felt queasy and her hands were shaking. She opened the door to the building that housed the special program and stepped inside. It was spacious and thank God it didn't smell like a hospital. She hated that smell. She looked around and saw several patients seated in different areas of the room. They were acting weird. Were these crazy people?

Lisa had been so deep in her musings that she jumped when she was greeted by a man and a woman who appeared to be in their mid-thirties. He was the first to speak.

"Hello, I'm Jeff Myers," he informed and then indicated the woman standing beside him. "This is Amanda Wheeler."

Lisa nervously smiled. "I'm Lisa Caulder." She was surprised when neither Jeff nor Amanda reached out to shake her hand.

"This, uh," Lisa again nervously eyed the patients in the room. "This wasn't what I was expecting."

Jeff offered her a cup of coffee and she took it.

"Why don't we sit down and we'll tell you all about what we do at the Group House and if you don't like what you hear, you're free to go," Jeff bargained.

"Really?" she asked, wide-eyed.

"Really," replied Amanda, smiling.

"It's just, I mean, I thought there would be people in white coats, crazy patients, straight jackets, shock treatment—that kind of stuff."

Jeff laughed. "Most people do. C'mon we'll tell you all about our program."

The three sat at a table and Jeff and Amanda told her all about the program.

"You see," Jeff started. "We deal with people who are struggling with emotional issues. We ask a lot of questions, mainly to get a better idea of what the real issues are. And we listen—*a lot*! We also encourage interaction with other participants, like building a network."

"Why did my attorney think I needed to be here?" she asked.

Amanda answered. "We don't know that you need to be here. We just want you to know the program is available to you. You received a severe blow to your head. An injury like that often leaves a person feeling edgy, irritable, and moody. Sometimes they have a hard time getting back to who they were before their injury."

That certainly described her, she thought.

Jeff added, "They also suffer from short-term memory loss, which can be very aggravating and cause anxiety."

Lisa offered a faint smile.

"Any of that sound like you?" Jeff asked.

"I do have problems with my short-term memory. And my husband says I jump at him all the time for no reason. I'm also very self-conscious about the way I look now."

"We can help you work through all of those." Amanda assured her.

Jeff took over. "We have a very structured program here. We start at 9:00 a.m. with group therapy. That's when we all get together and talk about what everyone's going through. How they're dealing with it; what works; what doesn't. Then at 11:00, we all have chores that need to be done. We have lunch around noon, which is prepared by the patients."

Amanda added her thoughts. "Depending on who's cooking, the meals range from tasty to let's-go-grab-something-from-the-vending-machine-instead."

Lisa smiled.

"After lunch, we have planned activities and then another group session."

Just then, a man who appeared to be the same age as Lisa walked over to the table where the three were seated. He looked at Jeff.

"You said you'd be gone only a few minutes."

"Give us a few more minutes, Charles," Jeff said.

"But you said you would talk to me!" the man replied.

Amanda stood. "Charles, this is Lisa. Lisa, I'd like you to meet Charles. Lisa will be joining our group."

"Hello," she said softly.

"But you said you would talk to me!" he yelled, ignoring the introductions.

Jeff stood and led Charles away. "Okay, Charles. Let's you and I go into the big room and we'll talk."

"I want both of you to come!" he demanded.

"I'll be there in a minute, Charles. I promise. I just want to finish talking to Lisa," Amanda said.

Charles became more agitated. He pointed a finger to Lisa. "It's *your* fault if I die!" He pulled free from Jeff's grasped and stormed out the door.

"Shouldn't you go after him?" Lisa asked.

"He'll be back," Jeff said. "He always comes back."

Jeff and Amanda led Lisa to the group that was now arranging their chairs in a circle. True to Jeff's word, Charles came back and joined the group. To bring the session to order, Jeff asked everyone in the group to introduce themselves one-by-one. Lisa was the starting point and she gave her name. By the time they went around the circle, she had forgotten everyone's name.

"Lisa, do you want to tell everyone why you're here?" Amanda asked.

She wasn't sure why she was here, but she softly told the group about her wreck. There were a couple groans and gasps as she told her story and it felt good to know they were actually listening to her words. Brian stopped doing that a long time ago.

"I used to be very pretty," she continued. "But I don't feel pretty anymore. When I married my husband, I was under this foolish notion that he was marrying me for me, and that my attractiveness was just a bonus for him. But I don't feel that way anymore. And now that my beauty is gone, he's no longer interested in me." She eyed the group. "Look at this face. It's not what you would call pretty."

Some of the group members had tears in their eyes, as though they felt her pain; others looked at the floor, almost too embarrassed to look at her face.

"My husband wanted to take me out for dinner on New Year's Eve. But none of my dresses fit me. I've lost so much weight. I used to have a nice figure. Anyway, we didn't go."

"There's so much more to you than your looks, Lisa," Amanda pointed out. "Do you like yourself?"

Lisa thought for a moment. "I liked the old Lisa, but I don't like who I am now. Sometimes I even hate myself."

"So what your saying, Lisa, is that your self-esteem and your feelings of self-worth are based on your looks?" Amanda asked, wanting to be sure she understood.

Lisa cocked her head. "Well, I never thought about it before, but I guess you're right."

"What we can do here, in this group, is help you find out who the real Lisa is. We can also deal with your anger."

Lisa nodded. "I am very angry and sometimes I don't know what do to with it. I always seem to take it out on my husband."

"That's understandable," Amanda pointed out. "He's the only person you come in contact with on a daily basis, right?"

Lisa nodded again.

"Sometimes, when we're angry, we take it out on those who are closest to us because it feels safer."

Lisa wasn't sure she understood what Amanda was saying, but she felt optimistic about the group.

"I'm anxious to find the real Lisa, too," she added.

"We're all glad that you're here, Lisa, and we're here to help you with these issues."

When they were done focusing on Lisa, others in the group had their turn at speaking and before Lisa knew it, the session was over and it was lunchtime. She was assigned kitchen duty with Charles and the two worked together to prepare the meal.

"Lisa," Charles finally broke the uncomfortable silence between the two of them as they worked side-by-side. "I just wanted to tell you that I accept you the way you are. I don't care about the way you look. You are a nice person."

She smiled. "Thank you, Charles." In a way, he reminded her of Peter, the photographer whom she worked with at the Sheraton back in Washington.

"I'm sorry if I was rude earlier," he continued.

"It's okay. I understand."

"I should tell you that I'm manic depressive and when I don't take my medicine, I get a little crazy. I had a great job in property management and was making a good income. When I lost my job, my wife left me. She would belittle me and tell me I was a worthless looser. I wanted to kill myself. Instead, they brought me here."

"I felt the same way after my accident," she opened up to him, surprised at her candor. "I thought life wasn't worth living. Brian, my husband, he wasn't emotionally available for me and I felt very alone. When we first married, he loved to show me off to his friends. Now he is ashamed of me."

"I know how that feels."

When they completed preparing the meal, everyone sat down to eat. After clean up, they returned to the group session. The day went by quickly.

At 5:00 p.m., Angie greeted Lisa as she exited the building.

"Well," her friend smiled. "How did it go?"

"Great. I really liked the group leaders and I think the group therapy will help me. Since I'm not working, it will force me to adhere to a schedule."

Angie couldn't help noticing that Lisa's step seemed just a little bit lighter and a little more bouncy. She was glad.

"I met this guy named Charles. We made lunch together and talked. We have a lot in common. He seems to understand how I feel."

Lisa continued to share the day's events with Angie but stopped abruptly when she'd spied a large empty parking lot alongside the road.

"Angie, are you in a hurry?" Lisa asked.

"Not really. What do you have in mind?"

Lisa's voice was a bit unsteady. "I-I haven't driven yet since the wreck. There's a parking lot." She turned to her friend. "Do you think we could stop there and let me drive around it a few times?"

Angie smiled. "Of course."

Angie pulled into the vacant lot and she and Lisa switched seats. Lisa's hands were sweaty and her heart raced. Her foot was shaking nervously on the accelerator. Good thing the car was still off.

Angie felt her apprehension. "Hey, why don't we just start with turning on the engine? You don't have to drive anywhere. Just turn the ignition."

Lisa loosened her grip on the steering wear and the color slowly came back to her face.

"Okay," she hoarsely responded and slowly turned the key. The engine started and she felt light-headed. "I don't think I can do this, Angie."

"We don't have to go anywhere," Angie reassured her. "Let's just sit here with the engine on and talk."

"Okay," Lisa agreed, feeling relieved. "Angie, can I ask you a question?"

"Sure."

"All of my other friends have abandoned me," she stated. "Why did you stick around?"

Angie smiled. "I have to tell you at times you did test my resolve to hang in there with you. You could be pretty mean when you wanted to be."

"I'm sorry."

"It's okay," Angie answered. "Anyway, the real reason is my sister."

Lisa looked confused.

"Do you remember when I told you my sister was in a car crash?"

Lisa thought for a moment and did recall the evening out when Angie shared that information over dinner. She also remembered how Stuart had rolled his eyes when Angie spoke of it.

"What I didn't tell you was that it was Stuart who was driving, and he was drunk at the time."

Lisa gasped.

Angie continued. "We moved to Atlanta shortly afterwards and I felt like I was abandoning my sister; I wasn't there for her when she needed me."

Lisa leaned over and gave Angie a hug.

"I appreciate everything you have done for me, Angie."

"You're like a sister to me, Lisa. I just want you to get better and be yourself."

Lisa wondered if she had *ever* been herself. Regardless, she forgot about her fear of driving and moved the gear from park to drive. She slowly accelerated and made three loops around the parking lot. Although she hadn't exceeded ten miles per hour, it was still a major accomplishment in her eyes.

"I did it!" She beamed, bringing the car to a halt. For a while, she'd been afraid that she would never be able to get behind the wheel. Brian kept pressuring her to drive again and when she would tell him she was afraid, he'd tell her to get over it. He didn't understand at all. Angie did.

The two girls switched places again and were on their way.

"Thank you, Angie," Lisa said. "I am very grateful for everything you're doing for me. Surely there's something I could do for you."

Angie smiled. "There is. How's your eyesight? Can you read any better?"

"It's hard at first, but my eye focuses after a few minutes."

"Up to grading papers from school? I'll have sixty midterm tests at the end of this week that need graded. I could use your help."

"I would love to!" Lisa replied. "I haven't felt as though I've been contributing to much of anything lately. I would really enjoy helping you grade papers."

Once inside, she put a pot of water on the stove for tea. When the kettle whistled, she removed it from the burner and tilted it over her teacup and began pouring. She completely missed the cup and the scalding water spilled over the table, the floor and even splashed on her. She flung the teapot against the wall and sank to the floor. She'd taken one step forward...and two steps back. She was just about to sink into her pool of self-pity when a voice deep inside her boomed, "NO!"

At first, she was frightened by the power of her inner voice. But it repeated itself again, "NO!" From somewhere deep inside of her, she was fighting back. She would not give into the self-pity she'd grown accustomed to the past few months. She would not give up. She would fight to rebuild her life.

The new feelings felt odd to her, but she clung to them. Her heart beat heavily in her chest and she took a couple of deep breaths to slow it. When she was feeling calmer, and more in control, she retrieved her diary.

"Emmit Hickson, you want a diary of my inadequacies? she asked aloud. "You're going to get so many diary pages from me you'll run out of filing space in your office!"

Her first entry: *Loss of depth perception.*

She then proceeded to clean up the mess she'd made.

Lisa's next step in her rehabilitative journey was getting braces on her teeth. She squirmed in the chair as the orthodontist adjusted the tension. She wasn't at all pleased to have to wear braces. She'd never worn them as a teenager; she'd been blessed with a set of perfectly straight teeth...until Walter Fowler entered her life.

Her mind wandered and she remembered, regrettably, all the boys she had declined a date with in high school because they wore braces. She somehow found them flawed. Did that mean she was now flawed?

When the orthodontist was finished, the first thing out of her mouth was, "Can I still eat what I want? My husband is taking me out to dinner tonight."

The orthodontist smiled. "As long as your husband isn't taking you to a restaurant where popcorn in the main dish, you should be fine."

Lisa frowned. "I can't have popcorn?"

"No popcorn," he ordered. "The receptionist will give you a detailed list of foods and candies to stay away from."

She was disappointed. She'd finally graduated to solid foods and she was still being limited, this time because of the braces. She loved popcorn!

"How long will I have to wear the braces?"

"About three years."

No popcorn for three years? She'd already been eight months without it. "I don't think I can do this, Dr. Matthews."

"You'll be fine, Lisa. You'll adjust; it just takes a little time. I have faith in you."

On the ride home with Brian, she calculated how many days she would have to go without popcorn. One thousand and sixty-eight days. She wondered what pureed buttered popcorn would taste like.

That evening, Brian and Lisa met up with Angie and Stuart at a nice Italian restaurant. Lisa was glad to be out.

"I didn't realize it would be so hard to eat with braces," Lisa announced, no longer trying to eat but instead playing with the food on her plate. "My teeth hurt."

"You'll get used to it," Angie responded. "I'm glad we got together this evening. It feels like old times."

Stuart lifted his wine glass. "To old times, and to Lisa, our miracle girl. You've come a long way and we're proud of you."

Everyone lifted their glasses to the toast before drinking.

"I have come along way," Lisa agreed. "Hey, did you hear that? I actually said something positive about myself."

Angie smiled. "Maybe your group therapy visits are paying off."

"Could be," she replied and turned to Brian. "What do you think, honey?"

Brian swallowed the rest of the wine in his glass before he responded. "I think Angie's the eternal optimist."

The four became silent. No one knew what to say. No one was quite sure what Brian meant by his comment. Lisa was the first to find her voice.

"What does that mean?"

Brian looked at her across the table; she looked hurt. He looked at Angie; she was scowling.

"Yes, Brian," Angie added. "I would be very interested to know what you mean, too. It seems kind of ridiculous that you think you know more about Lisa's progress than I do, since it's usually me who takes her to her appointments and takes her to practice driving."

Brian stuck his foot in his mouth and he knew it. He tried to recover. "I'm just concerned for your welfare, Lisa. I want to make sure we don't pump you up instead of being realistic."

"I think in this situation, Brian," Angie spoke firmly, "a little bit of praise is healthy." She looked at Lisa. "You are doing a superb job, Lisa, and I'm very proud of you."

Stuart added his thoughts. "I'm with Angie. I see progress in you every day and you smile more."

Lisa blushed.

Brian became defensive. "Hey, this is a tough world. I just think if Lisa's going to make it, she ought to become tough and not expect praise for doing what's expected of her."

"Brian you can be a real jerk," Stuart said.

Brian had too much to drink and he knew it. But that didn't stop him from responding to Stuart. "If I were a real jerk, Stuart, I would have told you what I was really thinking, which is Lisa made it through life on her looks, not her brains."

Lisa gasped. The table became silent for a moment.

Lisa took the napkin from her lap and placed it on the table. "What you're really saying, Brian, is that I've lost my *face value*."

When he didn't respond, she wished the floor would open up and swallow her, but only for a moment. "Furthermore, What I really have to face, Brian, is the fact that you married me for my looks and not for who I am."

Brian felt the icy stares from Stuart and Angie. He looked at his watch and said, "We need to get going. Lisa needs her rest."

"I'm not tired," Lisa informed him, her anger now apparent.

"Well, I have a meeting in the morning, so let's go," he told her. He stood and took her elbow to help her up.

Angie knew that Brian had too much to drink. "Brian, why don't you let us drive you home and you can pick up your car tomorrow."

"I'm just fine to drive," Brian shot back.

"You've had too much to drink, Brian," Stuart assessed. "Angie's my designated driver, you might as well let her be yours, too."

Lisa gently touched his arm. "Brian, let Angie drive us home."

Brian finally relented.

Chapter Ten

Lisa shielded the midmorning sun from her good eye while sitting on the carpeted floor at the group house. Jeff and Amanda, and the rest of the group participants were listening intently as Lisa filled them in on last night's drama.

"When I was pretty, I had a great job, lots of friends, and a wonderful husband," Lisa shared. "When I lost my beauty, I lost my job, my friends, and I'm slowly losing my husband. He only married me for the way I looked."

"Why did you marry him?" Jeff asked.

Lisa searched for the answer and lowered her gaze when it came. "Because he was attractive and successful...I guess I was superficial, too."

"Lisa," Amanda spoke up. "You need to go deep within yourself and learn to love and appreciate you for who you are."

"Some people spend their entire lives searching for happiness outside themselves and they never find it—because it doesn't exist," Jeff added.

"You and I have talked many times, Lisa," Amanda said. "I can already see your inner beauty."

"Brian doesn't."

"He probably doesn't know how," Jeff said. "But you shouldn't let that stop you from loving yourself and recognizing your beauty."

Amanda addressed the entire group. "I think we're going to stick with Lisa's theme today, since it applies to many of us. We're going to talk about self esteem."

"When you are depressed," Jeff began, "you automatically believe you are worthless. A recent study revealed that eighty percent of depressed patients didn't like themselves. That's a pretty high number and an awful feeling to have—especially since you're the one person you spend the most time with."

Everyone in the group laughed.

"When you're depressed," Amanda said, "you feel defeated, defective and deserted."

"I feel all of those!" Lisa shared.

"Since most of you feel that way, Amanda and I are going to talk to you about how to overcome it. It's difficult, and it takes a lot of time and energy at first, but the rewards make it all worthwhile."

"The first thing you need to do," Amanda said, "is train yourself to recognize your negative self-talk, also known as your critical thoughts. When you recognize it, write down on a piece of paper what it's saying to you."

"What if we run out of paper," one of the group members humorously asked. At that, everyone laughed.

"We promise if you do these exercises faithfully, there'll be no need to run out of paper," Amanda assured the group.

Jeff took over. "You need to learn why these thoughts are distorted and for that, we have a handout that lists all the distortions. After you write your negative thought down, you're going to immediately identify it."

"Once you've identified it," Amanda said, "You're going to learn how to talk back to your negative or critical voice and eventually disarm it until it becomes a whisper that you rarely hear. We want you to develop a more realistic self-evaluation system."

"Lisa, let's start with you," Jeff suggested. "When you tell yourself that you're ugly, you create and feed your feelings of despair. If you were to begin saying positive things about you to yourself, you would soon believe them—and so would others."

"I don't buy that," said one of the guys from the group.

"That's good, Tom," Amanda pointed out. "And I would advise the rest of you to learn something from Tom's skepticism. Never buy into anything Jeff or I say, until you've checked it out. If you try what we say, and it doesn't work for you, then you are justified in your disbelief. However, if you conclude it doesn't work without trying it, then you're still listening to that critical voice."

"Make the first step you take outside these doors today a new one," Jeff said. "When you leave today, monitor your self-talk, and start saying good things about yourself."

Lisa hung on their every word and couldn't wait to leave today to try what they were suggesting. She was like a piece of clay just waiting to be molded.

The date of her next surgery rolled around and she had butterflies in her stomach as she packed her overnight bag. At least Brian would be there, she thought, finding a little bit of comfort in that fact. Even though he couldn't be there in mind and spirit, he was there in presence. She should at least be thankful for that.

When he walked into the bedroom, she clutched her overnight bag at her midsection and said, "I'm ready."

"Uhm...I...uh something came up, Lisa," he mumbled, not bothering to look at her. "Do you mind catching a cab to the hospital?"

"I know I'm supposed to be a big, brave girl, and all that, but I would feel better if you would—"

"Hey, it's just another little operation. It's not like you haven't been through this before."

"That's not the point," she countered. "I want you...I need you to be there with me. I don't care how 'little' the operation is. You're my husband and I need your support."

Brian muttered something about how his support was paying for her medical bills. He left the room and made sure to slam the door behind him. He'd do whatever it took to provoke an argument this morning to get out of taking her.

Lisa's mind filled with negative thoughts and it took her only a second to recognize it. She took a cleansing breath and began to think positive things. I *am* worthy, she thought to herself. I won't let this bother me. This is Brian's issue—not mine. With that, she picked up the phone and called a cab.

During the cab ride to the hospital, she continued to say positive affirmations to herself. She was a strong person and she would survive.

Brian hummed a merry tune as he packed up his belongings from his office. A colleague entered his office and looked bewildered.

"What are you doing, man?" Wally Jacobs asked. Wally had curly red hair that earned him the nickname "Red" among his colleagues.

"What's it look like, Red?" Brian asked.

"It looks like you're packing up your office. Rich uncle croak and leave you a fortune?"

"Nope. Rich uncle didn't have to," Brian grinned from ear-to-ear. "My wife's going to make me a rich man."

Red, like everyone else in Brian's office, knew about the drunk driver that hit Lisa and the pending lawsuit. Personally, Wally thought Brian had been acting like an immature jerk for the past few months.

"You amaze me, Brian," he said with disdain before leaving the office.

"How are you feeling?" the nurse asked Lisa as she started to come out of the anesthesia.

"I'm in more pain this time than the last time," she said groggily. "Can I get something for it?"

The nurse retrieved some pain medication and raised her a bit so she could swallow the pills. It was difficult though, her entire face was bandaged.

She finally managed to swallow them and asked, "Does Dr. Howden think the surgery went well?"

"He seems pleased with the results."

"So we wait until the bandages come off?" she asked.

"We wait," the nurse repeated in a compassionate voice.

Lisa put her head on the pillow and drifted off to sleep.

Brian fluffed the pillows on his side of the bed before laying back. He opened his arm for her to curl up closer to him and she did so. He wrapped his arm around her and placed a butterfly kiss on her cheek. She smiled.

It was then he noticed the picture of Lisa on the nightstand. The woman lying beside him followed his eyes to it.

"Is that your wife?" Sissy asked. She'd met Brian a few weeks ago at a bar and the two had been sleeping together every chance they could. This morning when he called her to come over had been an unexpected surprise.

He nodded, surprised that he didn't feel any guilt.

"She's very pretty," she said. Pretty probably wasn't a strong enough word, Sissy thought. Gorgeous was more like it. She wondered what Brian was doing cheating on his wife with someone like her.

"I don't get it," she said. "Why are you stepping out on her?"

Brian shifted to reach over and open the nightstand drawer. He pulled out a photograph of Lisa after the collision.

"How's that for a reason?" he asked dryly.

Sissy's eye's widened. "That's the same woman?"

"She was hit by a drunk driver," Brian explained.

Sissy shrugged and curled close to Brian again. "Her loss is my gain," she purred.

The following morning, Dr. Howden checked on Lisa. He smiled as soon as he entered the room and saw she was awake. "How's my patient this morning."

Lisa returned the smile. "The pain isn't as bad. I'm feeling much better."

"Good. We'll just leave everything the way it is for a couple of days and then we'll take off the bandages and see if I'm worth my weight in gold."

She smiled. "Is there a money back guarantee if you're not?"

He smiled back. He was genuinely relieved to see she appeared happier, more confident, and more independent.

"Don't forget, there'll be some bruises when we first take off the bandages."

"But not as bad as last time, right?"

"No. Not as bad as last time," he assured her. "Now, get some rest and I'll check in with you later."

Lisa closed her eyes and began to repeat positive statements in her mind. The more she said them, the more she believed them and the easier they came to her. The critical voice was not as loud as it had been before she started group therapy and she was able to easily identify it when it kicked in. Before she knew it, she had drifted off to sleep feeling fairly positive considering everything.

Two days later, the nurse's attempts to try to reach Brian at home continued to fail. The bandages were scheduled to come off today and she wondered why Lisa's husband wouldn't want to be here. It really didn't matter to her because she hadn't liked the man from the moment she met him, but he should at least be here for his wife's sake.

"Well," Dr Howden began. "Are you ready, Lisa?"

She was feeling a bit nervous but replied, "I'm ready."

With the nurse's help, he began to peel away the bandages. Lisa kept her eyes on his, looking for any telltale signs as to the success of the operation. He smiled and handed her a mirror.

She hesitantly took the mirror and slowly brought it to her face. She looked at herself and although she still didn't consider herself pretty, she looked much better than she did a few days ago when she checked in. There was still some bruising and some puffiness; she knew it would be a couple of weeks until she'd really know what she looked like.

Dr. Howden suspected she was a little disappointed and was maybe expecting a miracle. "Lisa, you do recognize how far you've come, don't you?"

She nodded.

"Your road to a complete recovery is getting shorter every day. Just keep taking the days one at a time and eventually, you'll get to a place where you can look back on all this and recognize it for what it is."

She wasn't sure she understood what he was saying, but she was anxious to leave and didn't pursue the conversation with him. Angie was waiting for her.

Lisa was still tired during the drive to her condo and didn't talk much. Angie did most of the talking. One thing was for certain, neither one mentioned Brian. Angie wasn't quite sure how things were between the two, but figured if Lisa wanted to talk about it, she would bring it up when she was ready.

Angie carried her overnight bag to the bedroom and Lisa trailed behind. Once inside her bedroom, she pulled the covers back to crawl into bed and she was surprised to find a pair of black panties beneath the covers. They weren't hers. She flung them across the room then looked into Angie's compassionate eyes. Yes, Angie would understand what Lisa was feeling.

Brian walked into the room. "How's my favorite girl?" he asked.

Lisa toughened up. "Well, who would that be Brian? Me? Or would it be the woman who was wearing those panties?" She pointed across the room to where they lay on the floor.

Brian tensed. Damn that Sissy! She probably did that on purpose. He stalled for time.

"What are you talking about, babe?"

Before Lisa could respond, Angie set the overnight bag on the floor and interrupted them.

"I need to get going, Lisa." She gave her a hug and left the condo.

"Who do they belong to, Brian?"

"I don't know who they belong to. Somebody must be trying to set me up, babe."

"I don't believe you."

"It's not what you think," he lied. All he could think of was that she would walk out on him and take her settlement with her.

"I didn't think you could stoop any lower," she said, surprised that she didn't feel anything. She felt numb.

He snapped his finger. "I know what must have happened. When I went out of town, I told Red he could crash here. His apartment is being painted and the fumes were bothering him." Brian checked her eyes to see if she was buying any of it. "Obviously, he brought someone back here for the night."

Lisa didn't know what to say.

Brian picked up the phone. "I'll call Wally right now and ask him if you want." He knew she would feel foolish and decline his offer.

"That's not necessary, Brian."

"Lisa," he scolded. "You don't really think I could make love to another woman in our bed, do you? I could never do that to you. I love you."

The more he spoke, the more confused she became. Her feelings were conflicted and she could hear both the positive and negative voice inside her head. She thought her head was going to explode.

Brian opened his arms to Lisa. "Come here, babe."

She slowly moved toward him and allowed him to put his arms around her.

The following morning, Brian decided to make a breakfast of French toast and bacon for Lisa. He needed to make sure she believed him about Red staying at their condo while he was on his "business trip." He also needed to convince her of his unwavering love until they received the settlement. He wasn't walking away empty-handed, that was for sure.

She was surprised to find him making breakfast when she entered the kitchen. He moved through the kitchen at a fast pace, trying to time the bacon with the French toast. In between flipping the slabs of French toast, he made fresh-squeezed orange juice and brewed coffee.

"Good morning, sleeping beauty," he greeted her.

"I see you made breakfast," she acknowledge, tightening the belt of her navy blue bathrobe. She took a seat at the table and Brian placed the hot food on the table.

When she didn't immediately dig in, he coaxed her, "C'mon, dig in! You deserve this for all the great strides you've been making lately."

He sat next to her and took a sip of his coffee. She finally placed some food on her plate and cut it into tiny pieces so that it was easier to eat.

He placed his hand on hers and managed to bring some tears to his eyes. "I know this is tough on you, babe. But we can make it through this together. And after this epicurean delight, I have a surprise for you."

Lisa didn't show any excitement, but she did wonder what the surprise was.

"What is it, Brian? Another pair of someone else's panties in our bed?"

He ignored her comment. "I'm going into business for myself."

Lisa coughed on her French toast. After taking a swallow of orange juice she asked, "You're what?"

"I have something to show you, too." He took her hand and walked her outside. Parked in their designated parking space was a brand new Mercedes 350 SL.

"Why did you buy a new car?" she asked, wide-eyed.

"When I quit my job, I had to give back the company car. I always wanted a Mercedes. I didn't see the harm."

Lisa was speechless. Did Brian have any more surprises for her?

Chapter Eleven

Brian pulled his new Mercedes into the parking lot of the fashionable new office building located in Buckhead, the most prestigious business district in the Atlanta area. After turning off the engine, he got out and went to the passenger's side of the car and opened the door for Lisa. She was scowling when she got out. She immediately disliked the building.

They walked into a plush office expensively decorated with cherry furniture, exquisite paintings, and exotic plants.

"Brian, can we afford this?"

"It's not really a question of can we afford this," he dodged her question. "It's more of can we afford not to? You can't make any real money working for anyone but yourself." He saw she was still scowling. "Sure it's a gamble, but what isn't these days?"

"Wouldn't it have been better to wait until this mess I'm going through is over? Why couldn't you wait?"

"This is the perfect time, honey. Trust me, you'll see."

Lisa thought for a moment. "Maybe I could help out here. I could answer phones or something like that."

"No, that wouldn't be a good idea," he immediately rejected her offer.

"Why?"

"I'd feel like you were checking up on me every day."

She arched an eyebrow. "Is there a reason I should be checking up on you daily?"

"No, but I know how paranoid you can get."

Lisa didn't know which she was feeling more of: hurt or anger. Regardless, she didn't say a word on the drive home.

At Lisa's next group therapy session, she hung onto each and every word being spoken. Finally, it was her turn to sit in the center of the group and share. She took her place.

Amanda scanned the faces of the participants and saw a genuine caring in each of their faces. She was delighted that the group members were growing so close. She was also thrilled to see Lisa coming out of her shell and bonding with others in the group.

"My husband is cheating on me," Lisa shared with everyone. "He says he's not, but I stopped believing his words weeks ago."

"How do you know he's cheating?" Amanda asked.

Lisa thought for a moment. "It's kind of a feeling in my gut. It's strange, I can't explain it. It's like my head wants to believe his words, and sometimes I still do, but my gut knows the truth whether my head wants to admit it or not."

Amanda smiled. "You're very wise, Lisa. Sometimes we try to process what goes on around us with only our head. We rationalize, we discredit, we tend to listen to an outside source instead of acknowledging what we know in our 'gut' to be the truth. And then when we realize down the road that our gut had been right all along, we get angry that we didn't trust ourselves."

"I understand what that means now," Lisa replied. "I am now able to look back over my marriage and recognize the times when I knew in my gut that Brian was lying to me, but I chose to believe his words instead. And each time I chose to believe his words over my gut, my self esteem dropped just a little bit more."

One of the group members fidgeted. "I'm confused. How do I know what is coming from my gut and what is coming from my head?"

"That's a good question, Ed," Jeff said. "And there's no solid answer other than you just know."

"When you're in touch with your intuition, or your gut," Amanda began, "you become wiser. It's a defining shift that takes place inside of you, and once it occurs, you don't question it—you know it."

"There's a saying that goes '*The longest journey you'll ever make is the one from your head to your heart*'," Jeff added. "When you understand that saying, you're there."

"I'm getting confused," Louise said. "You're talking about the gut and intuition. Which is which?"

Everyone laughed.

"They are pretty much the same. People just have different names for them," Amanda explained. "It's more of a concept. For example, when you love someone with all your heart, your heart's not really loving them. You are. Not your head, not your heart, but you."

As the others continued to ask for more explanation, Lisa turned her thoughts inward. She did understand the statement about the longest journey. She'd been on that journey since the first day after the wreck and didn't even know it!

The focus of the group turned back to Lisa.

"Lisa," Amanda began. "You said you know that Brian's cheating on you. How does that make you feel?"

Tears lined her eyes as she got in touch with the pain of betrayal. "It hurts."

"Do you think you deserve to be in an unfaithful relationship?" Jeff asked.

"After my car crash, I would have said yes. I was so dependent on Brian and couldn't do anything for myself. I needed him even if he was cheating. As long as he stayed, I didn't care what he did. I just didn't want to be alone. I couldn't make it on my own."

"And now?" Amanda asked.

"I feel emotionally stronger now," she replied. "In some ways I feel stronger than I did *before* the wreck."

"Good for you, Lisa!" Jeff said.

One by one she looked at the faces of everyone in the group. "I could not have done it without everyone here."

"Have you and Brian talked about seeing a marriage counselor?" Amanda gently asked.

"He won't go," she replied. "Part of me wants to leave him, but I'm afraid to be on my own."

"You can overcome that fear," Jeff told her. "Human beings are born with only two natural fears: the fear of falling and the fear of loud noises. All other fears are learned and can be unlearned."

"Fear is at the root of many of the problems we all struggle with," Amanda added. "It ruins our relationships and often keeps us 'stuck.' For example, when you have a fear of rejection, you naturally wear a mask and pretend to be something you're not because you fear if anyone saw the real you, they'd reject you. The same goes for the fear of abandonment."

"Does anyone see how much of your energy it takes to 'be someone else?' You have to continually be on guard to make sure the real you never shines through."

Lisa understood what she was hearing. There were many times, even before the wreck, when she wouldn't share things with Brian for fear of what he would think of her. At some point, she simply learned to say and do what he expected of her.

"Lisa," Amanda spoke. "Do you think you're strong enough to let Brian know how you really feel? No matter what the consequences?"

The bell rang indicating the end of the session.

She reread the statement from the bank. There had to be a mistake. The last statement showed them having thousands in their account. How could there be so little in the account now? She nervously dialed the number to the bank and was placed on hold several times until someone answered who was finally able to help her.

"Mrs. Caulder," the voice on the phone said. "We're showing that the money was withdrawn on two separate occasions by Mr. Caulder."

"But this is a joint account! How could he withdraw so much money without my signature?"

"Well," there was silence for a moment. "It looks like the account you and your husband share was changed from an account requiring both signatures for a withdrawal to one where only one signature was required."

Lisa went numb. Brian must have forged her name on documents to change the type of account they had. She hung up the phone without saying goodbye.

She patiently waited for Brian to return from work. When he walked in and saw her stone expression, he knew he'd been caught at something. He just wasn't sure what.

"We got the bank statement in the mail today."

"I told you I would take care of the finances," he told her.

"What finances?" she shot back. "There isn't any money in the account."

"I needed to juggle some money around to pay for my car and new office."

"Brian, how could you? That money was from the insurance company and was supposed to pay for my doctor bills." Not only was he cheating on her, now he was stealing from her. Amanda's question was ringing in her ears. *Do you think you're strong enough to let Brian know how you really feel? No matter what the consequences?*

Yes, she thought. She was strong enough. She would not allow herself to be paralyzed by fear any longer.

"Brian, I'm leaving you," she said softly, but determinedly.

His mouth hung open. "You can't do that!"

She ascended the steps to the second floor with him at her heels.

"Lisa, I love you. I need you," he assured her.

She could feel the shift taking place inside her. Although she heard his words in her mind, her gut knew they were empty and meaningless.

"You don't know what love is, Brian." She entered the bedroom and retrieved a suitcase from the closet. She wasn't sure where her strength was coming from, but she was going to go with it and not question it.

He tried to grab the suitcase from her. The icy glare she gave him told him she wasn't bluffing.

She retrieved items from her bureau and neatly placed them in her suitcase. "I know you've been cheating on me, Brian, and I refuse to be the victim any more."

Brian began to panic. "Lisa, c'mon. We can work things out."

She looked in his eyes and was surprised to really see him for the first time. There was no love or compassion in his eyes; instead she saw a window to a cold and selfish heart. Such irony, she thought. She was now blind in one eye, but could finally see clearer than she had when she'd had both eyes. Ironic indeed.

Angie and Stuart were watching television when the doorbell rang.

"Who could that be?" Stuart asked.

"I don't know, but you're closer to the door," she grinned. "You get it."

Stuart headed to the door while keeping one eye glued to the television. When he reached the door, he swung it open and was surprised to find Lisa standing there.

"Lisa! What are you doing here?" He looked past her. "Is Brian with you?"

"No," she softly replied. "It's just me."

It was then he spied her suitcase. He reached down and picked it up for her. "Come in."

Angie came to the door and was surprised to see her friend. "Are you okay? Where's Brian?"

"No Brian," she replied. "Just me."

Angie wrapped her arm around Lisa's shoulder. "What happened? You look like you've been crying."

They moved to the living room and took a seat.

"I've left Brian," she informed her friends.

Neither Stuart nor Angie was surprised. In a way, Angie was glad.

"Stuart, can you put some hot water on for tea?" she asked her husband.

"Sure." He stood, but before leaving the living room, he gave Lisa a hug. "You're always welcome here, Lisa."

"Thank you, Stuart. I needed to hear that."

When Stuart was gone from the room, Angie took Lisa's hand. "Tell me what happened."

Chapter Twelve

After waiting almost two years, Lisa's day in court finally arrived. She wasn't involved in the proceedings; Hickson wanted it that way. His strategy was to have the jury hear all the testimony and then have her enter the courtroom to give her testimony on the last day. The jurors would be shocked by her appearance and *that* would win them over.

Her mother and sister, Diana, had flown to Atlanta and occupied much of her time while the hearing took place. She was nervous, but somewhat thankful that she didn't have to be in the courtroom hearing what everyone was saying. It might dampen her spirits to hear how those people closest to her compared her old self to the person she was now.

"All rise," the bailiff directed. "The court in and for the county of Cherokee is now in session. The Honorable Waldo C. Squires presiding."

After the judge was situated on the bench, the jury was directed to resume their seats.

"Case number C1473288, Lisa Caulder versus Kinderland Auto Sales and Walter Fowler."

"I see counsel for the plaintiff and for the defendant. Since the jury has been decided upon, I assume we are ready to go. Is that correct, Mr. Hickson?" the judge asked.

"Yes sir, your Honor."

"Fine, you may proceed."

Hickson began his opening argument. "With very little effort, I intend to show this court conclusive proof that the defendant Kinderland Auto Sales is libel for certain actions that resulted in my client Lisa Caulder suffering tremendous bodily and emotional injury."

Hickson eyed the jurors before pouring himself a glass of water.

"Your Honor, and ladies and gentlemen of the jury, I will show that Kinderland Auto Sales was grossly negligent. They allowed an employee to drive a company-owned vehicle while under the influence of a drug."

The first well-dressed defense attorney jumped up. "Objection, your Honor."

The judge was baffled. "To what?"

"To the word 'drug.' The alleged employee at the time of the accident showed a blood alcohol level of .22. That would signify him being well above the legal limits of intoxication, but not under the influence of a drug."

"Sustained." The judge nodded toward the court recorder. "You will strike the word 'drug' from the record." He looked at Hickson. "Please alter your terminology, Mr. Hickson."

"The driver, Walter Fowler, was well above the legal limits of intoxication," Hickson restated.

There was no objection from the defense team.

"Now that we have established one side of the litigation, I would like to establish the other. My client Lisa Caulder enjoyed a rather lucrative position as catering sales director of a large hotel chain. Her future looked bright until that Saturday morning."

The hearing dragged on that first day, with the defense setting a record for objections, most of which were overruled.

The following day in court, there was a large easel set up in the middle of the court room. It remained covered until Hickson took the floor.

"Yesterday, during my opening arguments, you heard me describe the collision, my client, and so forth. But I think Confucius was most correct when he said something about a picture being worth a thousand words."

He lifted the cover on the easel and revealed a blown up photograph of the mangled BMW Lisa had been driving that day. The jury gasped. The object in the photo didn't even resemble an automobile; it looked more like a crushed tin can.

"When looking at this mass of twisted metal, you are perhaps wondering how anyone could have lived through this horrible crash." He paused for effect. "It was purely by the grace of God, I assure you."

He removed the photo of the BMW and situated behind it was a picture of Lisa before the wreck. She was smiling and looked absolutely radiant.

"This, ladies and gentlemen, is a photograph of my client taken a few months before the collision. And this," he said as he removed that photo to reveal the next, "was how she looked in the hospital the day following the horrible car crash."

He noticed the horror on some of the faces of the jurors; others chose to look away from the grotesque sight. Regardless, they all were repulsed by what they saw.

One of the defense attorneys leaned over to another and whispered, "Aren't you going to object?"

"On what grounds?"

Hickson called his first witness to the stand.

"Please state your name and your profession."

"Lawrence Clayton. I'm an emergency room physician at Northridge Hospital."

"Did you remember treating Lisa Ann Caulder in the emergency room at Northridge Hospital?"

"Yes, sir."

"You were the first physician that treated her, is that correct?"

"Yes."

"What was her condition when she arrived in the emergency room at Northridge?"

"The major concern when she came into the emergency room was her central nervous system injury of an undetermined nature. The blunt force she took to the face and head put her in a critical condition. The facial injuries, although severe and cosmetically disfiguring were not my primary concern. It was her central nervous system that was greatly affected by her injuries. At one point, we could not get a pulse and we had to revive her. When we finally stabilized her vitals, we were concerned about the trauma to her brain."

"After your assessment, did you call in any specialist?"

"I immediately called a neurosurgeon, an ophthalmologist, and a plastic surgeon."

"What else did you do for her at that time?"

"I started an IV and gave her medication to decrease the swelling in her brain."

"Could you describe for us what she looked like?"

"She came in with a very swollen face and with what we call raccoon eyes—a euphemism. Her face had taken such a blow that her eyes had swollen and turned black and blue from the bleeding under the skin. I could literally rock the bony part of the face free from the skull. Her eyes had what we call hypertelorism. That is a fancy word for the blow that is so severe to the face it moved her eyes outward. Both pupils were dilated and we thought she was blind in both eyes at first."

"Thank you, Dr. Clayton. That is all for now."

Hickson was pleased with Dr. Clayton's testimony. He turned to opposing counsel and said, "Your witness."

The three attorneys whispered among themselves before the lead looked at the judge. "The defense has no questions for the witness."

Hickson smiled, looked at his notes, and called his next witness.

"I would like to call Dr. Donald Traynor to the stand."

Dr. Traynor went up to the witness stand and was sworn in.

Mr. Hickson approached the Doctor. "Are you a licensed medical doctor in the State of Georgia?"

"Yes, I am."

"Are you engaged in any particular surgical specialty?"

"Yes, ophthalmology."

"Have you ever treated Lisa Ann Caulder?"

"Yes, I first saw her at Northridge Hospital."

"When you first saw her, was she conscious or unconscious?"

"She was unconscious."

"What was her condition when you saw her?"

"She had bilateral dilated pupils that did not react to light, and she had a hemorrhage in the anterior chamber of both eyes."

"What was the condition of her face?"

"She had multiple facial fractures, lacerations, and contusions."

"Did you suspect brain damage?"

"Yes, I did."

"Did you draw any significance or medical findings from these observations?"

"She did have brain damage and also the optic nerve was injured. I suspected she had glaucoma."

"Was the glaucoma due to the increased pressure in that eye?"

"Yes, it was."

"Is Mrs. Caulder now blind in her left eye due to that optic nerve damage?"

"Yes, she is."

"Does she also have problems with her depth perception?"

"Yes, her depth perception is reduced significantly. When you have two eyes, you get a sense that there are two views of one object in your environment and you are looking at it from two angles. When you only have one eye, everything looks flat."

"Is there anything known in the medical field that could restore the vision in Mrs. Caulder's left eye at this time?"

"No, nothing."

"No further questions."

The three attorneys again whispered among themselves and the lead attorney stood and asked some ridiculous questions trying to discredit the witness. Hickson could tell the jury didn't buy it.

Dr. Traynor left the courtroom and the judge called for a thirty-minute recess.

When the court convened, the three defense attorneys looked nervous. They could tell the expert witnesses had won over the jury.

The bailiff called the next witness and swore him in. Hickson walked confidently up to the stand to question him.

"Please state your name."

"My name is Michael Warrington."

"How long have you been licensed in the State of Georgia as a physician?"

"For over five years."

"Do you have a specialty?"

"Yes sir, neurosurgery is my specialty."

"Can you describe for us what the practice of neurosurgery is?"

"It is the diagnosing and treating of illnesses of the nervous system especially those that require surgery."

"In just plain old shirtsleeve English, might you be called a brain surgeon?"

"Yes, sir."

"Have you had an occasion to see a patient named Lisa Ann Caulder on an emergency basis?"

"Yes, I saw her in the trauma room at Northridge Hospital."

"Can you describe for the court her appearance at that time?"

"She had severe facial injuries and a brain injury. When I examined her, she had swelling of the face and what we call a mid-facial fracture, and her left eye did not respond to light."

"Did you perform a neurological examination on her?"

"Yes, sir."

"Can you tell the jury in simple terms what your examination found?"

"She had severe swelling of the face and was bleeding from every orifice—meaning her nose, mouth, ears, and eyes. When I looked into her left eye, I could see blood within the eye itself and the pupil did not respond to light which is an abnormal finding. I suspected that the eye would not recover and she would be blind. This was the case with Mrs. Caulder."

"What else did you find, Dr. Warrington?"

"Upon examining her, I found that she had what I call a free floating maxilla or mid facial fracture. This is when the face is broken free from the skull."

"Did you take x-rays?"

"Yes. When I took x-rays of the skull, there was what we call pneumocepalus. This means that air had gotten in the subarachnoid space between the brain and the skull. This could signify the potentiality of having severe infective problems. Luckily, she did not develop these."

"In your examination of her, did you find that she had brain damage?"

"Yes, she experienced minimal brain damage—she suffers from short-term memory loss. She additionally suffers mood swings, irritability, and difficulty concentrating."

"No further questions at this time."

Again, the defense asked a few lame questions that only seemed to offend the jury.

The judge called a recess for lunch. Hickson met with the other doctors and prepared his questions for the afternoon session.

The judge and jury entered the courtroom. "All rise."

After everyone was seated, Hickson put Dr. Howden on the stand.

"Please state your full name for the jury."

"John Allen Howden."

"How long have you been licensed medical doctor in the State of Georgia?

"Ten years."

"What does plastic and reconstructive surgery consist of?"

"Well, as pertains to this patient, one of the major things that a better plastic surgeon does is to reconstruct severe traumatic injuries, particularly to the face and head. Plastic surgeons will also do cosmetic surgery."

Dr. Howden, have you brought your hospital and clinical charts pertaining to Lisa here with you today?"

"Yes, I have."

"How did you first get called to Mrs. Caulder's case?"

"I was called by Dr. Michael Warrington when she was first admitted to the trauma room at Northridge Hospital. He called me because he was concerned, not only for her extensive brain injuries but also for her extensive lacerations and fractures of the bones of the face."

"Describe for the jury Mrs. Caulder's condition when you first saw her in the Northridge Hospital trauma room."

"She had the worst set of facial bone fractures, I have ever seen in anyone who survived. When I examined her, I could take her upper teeth and move the upper teeth forward and her whole face would move back and forth from her skull. She had soft tissue injury and she broke the bone that connects the cheekbone to the skull. This area was not fractured, it was pulverized. It was turned into powder. There were so many fractures of these bones that they felt like sand. Her nose was broken and her jaw was broken in three places. All of these fractures were extremely severe."

"So, her face was pretty much destroyed?"

"In all my years of practicing medicine, she was one of the worst cases I have seen."

"With all the plastic surgery known to man, will Lisa Ann Caulder ever look like she did before the collision?"

"Unfortunately, no. With all the bone loss she had, it would be impossible for anyone to reconstruct her face back to the way it was before the car crash."

Dr. Howden's testimony was very technical and lasted several hours. When he was finished the judge called for a short recess. When court reconvened, Hickson took center stage again.

"I have one last witness today, your honor. I would like to call the head nurse in the intensive care unit at Northridge Hospital. She was also an eye witness to the car crash. Kelly Brannigan."

Hickson was pleased with the trauma nurse's testimony…right down to the part where she described Walter Fowler's belligerence when he crawled out of his car after the wreck, nearly unscathed, while Lisa Caulder wasn't even breathing. The defense was stumped.

The following day, Lisa's best friend Sandra was to testify.
"Please state your full name."
"Sandra Elise Kennington."
"How long have you known Lisa Ann Caulder?"
"Lisa and I were college roommates. We have known each other for about seven years."
"Can you describe for us her general health before she was in the wreck?"
"She was in excellent health," Sandra answered then smiled. "She was very vivacious and full of life. I have never known her to be sick. I don't ever recall her ever having the flu."

"What type of personality did she have at that time?"

"She was very animated and loved people. She always enjoyed any type of new activity. She had a very out going personality."

"When did you first see Lisa after the collision?"

"I came down to stay with her when her husband Brian went out of town on a business trip. It was about a month after the wreck."

"Can you describe for the jury what her general condition was at that time?"

"She didn't look the same. Her big eyes were no longer almond-shaped and symmetrical. They were lopsided. Her left eye was off to one side and her nose was shorter and turned up. She had no bridge to her nose. Her face had a lot of swelling. Her mouth was wired shut and she could hardly talk. She did not look like the Lisa I knew."

"What about her breathing? Can you describe that?"

"She had a hard time breathing because she had a tracheotomy. She had a white patch of gauze over her throat. She was wheezing and I could tell she had difficulty breathing."

"How did she eat?"

"Not very well. I would fix her cream of wheat, but she could barely get it through the slits in her teeth and it had to be completely liquefied before she could ingest it."

"How long did it usually take her to eat her cream of wheat?"

"It took her over an hour to eat the complete bowl."

"What can you tell us about her sense of smell?"

"I made bacon one morning for me, and I left it on the burner too long. The house filled with smoke and it smelled of awful burnt bacon for hours. I apologized to her for smelling up her house and she told me not to worry about it—she couldn't smell anything."

"Was there anything she was able to do for herself while you were there?"

"No, she needed assistance in going to the bathroom, washing her hair, and bathing."

"How has her personality changed since the car crash?"

"Before, she was very positive and outgoing. She was full of energy. Now, she is consumed with taking care of injuries and is dependent on people. She doesn't have the energy to go shopping. When we do go out, she thinks people are staring at her because she is ugly. She also runs out of energy after about a half an hour."

"Has her appearance changed since the collision?"

"Yes, sir! Lisa had always been beautiful," Sandra's eyes filled with tears. "She never knew this but I was always envious of her looks." She wiped her eyes. "The first time I saw Lisa after the wreck, I didn't recognize her. It was like I was meeting someone for the first time. Everything I remembered about her was gone."

The judge saw that Sandra was getting emotional. He asked the bailiff to get her a glass of water and then called for a recess.

Next, Angie took the stand.

Hickson began the questioning.

"How has Lisa changed since the collision?"

"She really gets irritated and is short tempered now. She would never snap at me and always listened to what I had to say before. She also has trouble making decisions and is always confused. She had a great job as catering sales director and was always making major decisions at her work. It bothered her that she couldn't make a simple decision after the car crash."

Stuart took the stand.

"Can you tell the jury what type of person Lisa Caulder was before the collision?"

"Lisa was a very confident person. She was full of life. She was always smiling, independent, and a very hard worker. She was a beautiful young lady."

"Tell us how she is now."

"Since the wreck, Lisa is like a different person. She doesn't feel like anybody likes her anymore. She has no self-confidence. I mean if you can, imagine what it must be like for a person to be afraid to walk into a room because she thinks everyone is staring at her."

The defense attorney jumped up.

"Your honor, I hesitate to object, but I believe the witness is testifying about the state of mind of somebody else."

Judge Squires replied, "I will sustain the objection."

Throughout Stuart's testimony, the defense attorneys objected.

After a full day of testimony, the Judge called it a day.

Lisa sat at a local coffee shop with Stuart and Angie. "Thank you both for testifying for me. I am glad this trial is almost over."

Stuart being the life of the party always had a joke to tell. He felt now was the time to tell a few.

"Hey, Lisa, I have some lawyer jokes for you."

"I need to laugh right now. Tell me the jokes."

Stuart told several jokes about attorneys, some were funny and others were a bit off color.

When he had finished, Lisa laughed out loud for the first time in a long time.

Chapter Thirteen

Lisa was sitting on the guest bed leafing through her old journals and pictures when Angie tapped on the door.

"Come in, Angie."

"What are you doing?"

"I'm just getting some things together for court tomorrow."

Angie nervously bit her lip. "Lisa, I have something to tell you."

Lisa saw the pained look in her friend's face. "What's wrong, Angie?"

Angie moved to the bed and sat down next to Lisa. "This is hard for me to say, so I'm just going to say it. You remember me telling you that my mother is sick?"

"Yes, how is she now?"

"She's getting worse."

Lisa reached out and took Angie's hand. "Angie, I'm sorry."

"Stuart and I are moving back to Wilmington to take care of her."

"Oh no! Angie, what am I going to do without you?"

"You're going to fly solo, Lisa. That's what you're going to do."

"What are you talking about?"

Angie handed her the newspaper. "You're going to get a job and get your own place. It's time, you know."

Lisa's mind filled with panic, but only for a moment. She remembered what she learned in group therapy.

Angie continued. "You've been pouring your heart and soul into everyone you've met while volunteering at the soup kitchen. Now it's time you take that same dedication and apply it to yourself and get out there and find a job. You're strong, Lisa. You can do this."

She took the newspaper from Angie. "It's different. I feel good when I help others. Sometimes I think they need my help more than I do. Helping them kind of keeps me sane."

"Well, if you don't start helping yourself, you just may end up on the opposite side of the counter at the soup kitchen." Angie grinned. "They'll understand if you leave and maybe they can find hope through you. They know what you've gone through and how you fight every day to reclaim your life. The best thing you can give them is to show them how to reclaim their lives by reclaiming yours."

Lisa smiled—Angie had a point. "Well, maybe I am strong," she repeated her friend's words, "but that doesn't mean I'm not afraid."

"You'll do fine."

Lisa put her fear aside for a moment. "Angie, I'm going to miss you. You have been there for me so many times. I don't know what I'll do without you."

"I already told you," Angie smiled. "You're going to fly solo!"

The next day of the trial, Lisa and Brian testified. Lisa remained in the witness room while Brian testified. Hickson felt it best to keep the two separated so that Brian would feel more at ease and able to speak more freely about their situation—and maybe even indulge.

"Can you state your name for the court, please?"

"Brian William Caulder."

"Are you married to Lisa Ann Caulder?"

"Yes, I am."

"How long have you been married?"

"Two years. We were only married one year when the collision occurred."

"During the time that you lived with Lisa and up until the time of the wreck was she employed?"

"Yes, she was catering sales director at Bertonelli East."

"Had she had prior employment before that?"

"Yes. She worked at the Sheraton Park Hotel in Washington, D.C. as public relations assistant. And before that she worked at Bertonelli Capitol Hill. She was always career-driven."

"Can you describe the type of person Lisa was before the collision?"

"Lisa was a very energetic person, full of energy and a very lively person. She was very active, had a great personality, and was just fun to be with. She had a tremendous smile."

"How did you first learn about the collision your wife was involved in?"

"A police officer came to our home and told me she was in a car crash and that I should get to the hospital as quick as possible. He wouldn't tell me the extent of her injuries. I drove to the hospital, but I believed there was a mix-up. I figured Lisa was probably at work and they just made a mistake. When I got to the hospital, the doctor took me into a small room and told me her injuries. I still didn't believe it was Lisa until he handed me her wedding rings. It was then I knew it was really her."

"What did the doctor tell you about her injuries at that time?"

"Dr. Clayton told me that the bones in Lisa's face were shattered. He said her nose was broken and her jaw was broken in three places. The fractures were severe. He told me that he would have to wire her face back to her skull."

"What did she look like when you first saw her?"

"It did not look like her. She was black and blue. Her face was swollen to twice its normal size. Her eyes were swollen shut and she had a lot of blood on her. It looked like she had been beaten with a baseball bat."

"What was her condition when she left the hospital?"

"When Lisa first came home, she could not do anything for herself. I had to help her to the bathroom and help her with a bath. She had a bandage on her throat for the tracheotomy and her mouth was wired shut. It was difficult for her to talk. She was on liquids for three months. Soups had to be put in the blender because they were too thick and everything had to be watered down. She was in a lot of pain those first few weeks."

"How is she today?"

"She is not physically well. I thought that after the collision she would bounce back in about three months or so. She did not. She constantly has pain in her left eye. Her bad eye tears all the time. Her pelvic bone is always hurting her. She does not look, or act, the same as she did when I married her."

"How does she look different?"

"Her eyes are deep set and round. Her left eye is lopsided. She used to have beautiful eyes, long and almond shaped. Her face is shorter and more rounded. Her nose is shorter and turned up. She just has a different face. She is not the same Lisa."

"What other types of problems does she now have?"

"She has a short-term memory problem. She forgets to turn off the oven or she will buy groceries at the store and forget to take them out of the cart and put them in the car."

"How is her self confidence?"

"She has very low self confidence. She basically hates herself and if anybody is around her for any period of time, she begins hating them, too."

"How is your sex life?"

"She is not able to have sex without pain and crying. Before the collision, our sex life was great. Today it is bad and has been bad since then."

"Are there any other problems?"

"She has a problem with depth perception. It is hard for her to see steps. She fell one time we were at a restaurant. She also has a hard time pouring from a pitcher. We used to play tennis together. She was a good tennis player. Today she can't judge where the ball is and misses it. This frustrates her...and me."

"Has your marriage been affected?"

"Yes, sir. She thinks I don't love her. She thinks I loved the person she was before and not her now. I tell her that I love her but she doesn't believe me."

After Brian's testimony, it was Lisa's turn. The jury gasped when she walked in. Lisa entered the courtroom. She didn't look anything like the old Lisa they saw in the pictures. Her eye had gotten infected recently and was now swollen and red. Her face was round and her eyes were deep set and uneven. Her tan shirtwaist dress hung on her frail body. Although her short-cropped hair had grown out some, it wasn't as soft and bouncy as it had been before.

She went through her diaries and relived the last two years of her life for the jury. When the questioning began, her voice had been shaky, but finally leveled out. The jury hung on to her every word. It was clear they felt compassion for her. Some of them even scowled when the defense team's cross-examination was too brisk. The defense team was helping to sway the jury toward Lisa. There were only a couple of times when she broke down on the stand. After short recesses, she was able to compose herself and continue her compelling testimony.

When it was the defense team's time to cross-examine her, they did so harshly and won no points with the jury. This was a cut and dried case and they knew it.

The last day of the trial was reserved for the defense. They decided to put Walter Fowler on the stand.

Hickson questioned him.

"What is your full name?"

"Walter David Fowler"

"Looking back to the day of the collision, what is the first thing you remember after the crash?"

"I remember a blood sample being drawn."

"At the time of the collision, how long had you known Mr. Kinderland?"

"About twenty-two years."

"Isn't it true that prior to the time you were hired as a salesman at Kinderland Auto Sales, you and Mr. Kinderland were social acquaintances?"

"Yes."

"During the time that you were hired, and prior to this collision, did you ever have a discussion with Mr. Kinderland about the fact you did not have a valid drivers license?"

"Yes."

"Did you tell Mr. Kinderland that you didn't have a driver's license in your possession that was valid?"

"Yes."

"And did Mr. Kinderland tell you from time to time to do whatever you had to get the driver's license?"

"Yes."

"Did Mr. Kinderland know that your driver's license had been taken for bail due to a speeding charge?"

"Yes."

"Do you have a valid driver's license today?"

The defense attorney jumped up to object that the question was irrelevant and immaterial. The judge sustained the objection and instructed the jury to disregard the answer.

"Did you ever during the entire time you worked at Kinderland Auto Sales have a valid Georgia driver's license?"

"No."

"And did Mr. Kinderland and Mr. Bolen, the Sales Manager, know you did not have a driver's license?"

"Yes, sir."

"Isn't it true that you have driven under the influence many times and have never been caught?"

"Yes."

"During the time you worked at Kinderland Auto Sales you were separated from your wife, weren't you?"

"Yes."

"You often went bar hopping on Friday and Saturday nights. Is that correct?"

"Yes, sir."

"How many times have you been caught for DUI?"

"Three."

"And you have had a number of collisions, right?"

"Yes. I had four collisions."

"How many times has your driver's license been revoked?"

"Two times."

"Why was it revoked?"

"DUIs."

"Have you ever had an occasion to have an alcoholic drink on the premises of Kinderland Auto Sales?"

"Yes."

"How many times a week?"

"A couple of times a week."

"Did you ever drink alcohol on the premises with Ted Bolen, the Sales Manager?"

"Yes."

Hickson continued the questioning of Walter Fowler and then questioned Ted Bolen. The last to testify was Mr. Kinderland, the owner of the car dealership.

With all the testimony given, the judge instructed the jury on coming to a verdict. He then released them to deliberate.

The jury took eight hours to reach a verdict. Everyone was recalled to the courtroom. Lisa sat with her hands clenched, nervously biting her lower lip. Hickson was seated at the prosecutor's table doodling on his tablet. The judge entered the courtroom along with the jury.

"All rise. This court is now in session," the bailiff called loudly.

Judges Squires took his seat ready to proceed. He looked at the jury. "Mister Foreman, has the jury reached a verdict?"

"Yes sir, your Honor, we have."

"Please read the verdict," the judge directed.

"We the jury find the defendant Kinderland Auto Sales fully responsible through gross negligence and completely libel."

Lisa's shoulders slumped forward; she let out a heavy sigh. "Thank God," she thought to herself.

He read the amount awarded to Lisa and then sat back down with the other jurors. The other jury members didn't conceal their smiles; they were pleased they had struck a blow for the little person.

Lisa was in shock after hearing the high figure. She never dreamed it would be so much money. She eased back into her chair and allowed the tears to fall. These tears were tears of joy. The trial was over and she could start rebuilding her life.

Hickson was disappointed; he'd expected much more than that. He must have missed something along the way. Well, what's done is done, he thought.

The foreman of the jury walked over to her. He smiled and offered her kind words.

"We're sorry that you had to go through this, Mrs. Caulder. We hope that what we awarded you will at least help you begin a new life."

She smiled and thanked him.

"Can I give you a hug?" he asked, taking her by surprise. She reached out and hugged him.

"Thank you," she whispered again

The next day Lisa, her mom, and sister planned to celebrate over dinner, but the plans had to be changed at the last minute. The infection in Lisa's eye had gotten worse and required a trip to the emergency room. After three long hours of waiting, Lisa was taken to a small examining room.

"You have an infection and we need to lance the eye," the doctor informed her.

"Will it hurt?"

"There will be a little discomfort."

A little discomfort? When the procedure was over, Lisa was in so much pain she wanted to poke the doctor's eye with her finger and ask him if that's what he meant by a little discomfort!

He gave her a prescription for a powerful painkiller. After Lisa took the pain medicine, it made her so drowsy that the celebration dinner had to be cancelled.

The following day, Lisa's mother and sister boarded a plane for home. She knew what she had to do next.

Lisa was in the guest bedroom packing her things when a knock came at the door. It was Angie and Stuart.

"Hey, what's going on in here?" Stuart asked.

Lisa smiled. "Just packing my things. I found a couple of apartments I want to check out this afternoon." She looked at her suitcase. "I guess I'm being optimistic."

"Lisa, we don't have to be out of the house for three more weeks. Why are you packing now?" Angie asked. "I have a whole house to pack and I haven't even started yet!"

Lisa smiled at the two. "I appreciate everything the two of you have done for me. And I appreciate your offer to stay until you hand the keys over to the new owners, but I think I need to be by myself right now." Had she really said those words out loud? Be by herself?

Angie smiled. "I'm so proud of you, Lisa. You have come such a long way."

"I never thought I would get this far," she replied. "I could not have done it without you and Stuart. I owe you so much."

"You're like a sister to me, Lisa. You don't owe me anything."

"We've enjoyed having you," Stuart chimed in.

"I'm going to miss you both when you move to Wilmington."

The phone rang and Angie excused herself to answer it.

"Angie's right, Lisa. You've become part of our family and we're glad that we could be here for you."

His words touched her.

Angie entered the bedroom and handed her the phone. "It's for you. Sounds like Hickson."

Lisa took the phone and Angie and Stuart excused themselves from the room.

"This is Lisa," she said into the phone.

"Lisa, Emmit Hickson. How are you?"

"I'm fine, Mr. Hickson. Is something wrong?" She detected an edge in his voice.

"Well, ain't no easy way to tell you this so I'll just come right out and say it. The boys from Atlanta have appealed the case."

She was confused. "I don't understand. What does that mean? The jury found in my favor. They awarded me a settlement."

"Yes, they did," Hickson agreed. "But when it comes to lawsuits, wining is one thing, collecting is another."

"What happens now?"

"Best I can figure, those boys from Atlanta are going to drag this case out as long as they can. They'll try to wear you down and break you so you'll accept a deal just to end the aggravation."

"Well," she said firmly. "They thought wrong. I'm not accepting a deal."

"That's my girl. That's what I wanted to hear. You just leave it to me," he replied. "Oh, and since they're appealing, don't forget that my fee increases."

She groaned inwardly.

"You have a good day, Mrs. Caulder."

She hung up the phone and joined Stuart and Angie in the living room. She shared the bad news with them.

Angie reached out and took her hand. "Lisa, why don't you stay with us a couple more weeks?"

"I have to learn to deal with setbacks, Angie. And that's all this is—a setback."

Angie nodded and turned to Stuart. "Stuart, why don't you put some hot water on the stove for tea?"

"Sure, Angie."

Stuart left the living room and Angie led Lisa to the sofa.

"I was waiting for the right moment to tell you something," Angie started.

"What is it?"

"You keep thanking Stuart and me for everything we've done for you, but I want to thank you for what you've done for Stuart and me."

She was confused. "What have I done for the two of you?"

"Stuart quit drinking. He stopped on the day you moved in with us."

"Angie, that's wonderful!"

"I can't tell you how happy and relieved I am. He never would have stopped if it hadn't been for you. He's even going to AA meetings."

Lisa was genuinely happy for Angie and Stuart. She was making strides in her own life and was happy to know it was affecting others' lives in a positive way. She could tell the two had become closer.

"I never thought things would turn out like this," Angie shared. "I never thought I could feel joy in my relationship again and I do."

Lisa never thought things would turn out like this either. She wondered what tomorrow held for her...

Lisa boarded the midtown bus and continued reading the housing section of the newspaper. When she reached the location of the first apartment she was to see, she pulled the cord and when the bus came to a stop she exited.

She looked at the run-down brick apartment building situated before her and cringed. It was uninviting. She knocked at the door and the building superintendent answered. He looked just as bad as the building he lived in. His clothes were disheveled and there was a distinct odor coming from him that smelled like cigarettes and liquor. His face was unshaven and his hair was combed to one side to try to cover a significant bald spot.

"You here to see the apartment for rent?" he asked her.

She wanted to say no, that she'd made a mistake and knocked on the wrong door, but the fact she was still clutching the newspaper in her hand, and it was folded at the real estate section, made that impossible.

She toured the apartment and was disappointed and disgusted.

"A little paint and this will be good as new," the super guaranteed.

"A new what?" Lisa asked. There were holes in the wall, the ceiling was peeling, and there were a couple broken windows.

"Well, what do you expect for three hundred bucks a month? A penthouse view?" He led her to the window. "There, see that building across the street?"

She followed his gaze to the lovely apartment building located across the street.

"If you look at those top floors in the building across the street, there's your penthouse view!"

She didn't have time for this. She bid him good day.

She grabbed a burger from a fast food joint and sat on the bench at the bus stop eating her burger and reading more ads. She came across one with the heading "Nice apartment to share." She looked at her watch and knew she had a few minutes until the next bus came by. She ran to a nearby payphone and called the number in the ad.

A woman with a kind voice answered.

"My name's Lisa; I'm calling about the apartment you have listed in the paper."

"I'm Zoe," the voice responded. "Do you smoke, Lisa?"

"No."

"Do you have a drinking problem?"

"No."

"Do you have any irritating habits?"

Lisa was surprised when she laughed before answering, "No."

"Good," Zoe responded. "My phone's been ringing off the hook today with weirdos wanting to move in. You sound normal. Do you want to see the place?"

"Yes, I would."

Within a half hour, she found herself standing outside a nice apartment building in a better section of town. She knocked on the door and it was answered by a pleasant-looking woman with brown curly hair. She looked to be about twice Lisa's age.

After Zoe showed her around the apartment, she asked, "Well, what do you think?"

"I like it." It was nicely decorated; the furniture appeared old, but was in good shape. The apartment would do nicely until she settled her lawsuit.

"Your half of the rent is $250. Can you swing that?"

Lisa smiled. "When can I move in?"

"How does tomorrow sound?"

"Perfect!"

Lisa moved in the following day and things were great for the first two weeks. Then Lisa began to notice peculiarities in Zoe. The older woman wouldn't let her make long distance phone calls or use the stove. She then learned that Zoe was schizophrenic and had recently been released from a mental ward. Lisa suddenly realized she went from the frying pan into the fire.

She called Brian.

"How are you, Lisa," he responded, surprised to hear her voice on the phone. "I really miss you."

"I'm fine." She couldn't tell him how bad things were. Instead, she told him she'd found a great apartment and was sharing it with another woman.

"Would you like to have lunch," he asked.

"Yes, that would be great." She knew she was using him as a crutch, but she didn't feel she had any options right now.

They met at a steak house and he greeted her with a hug. "I'm so glad to see you, babe."

"I'm glad to see you, too, Brian," she wasn't sure if she really felt that way or not. She felt confused again. His words didn't seem to match his actions and she was reminded of the way she felt prior to leaving him. She knew he'd been having affairs, yet he never confessed to them. He would never confess to them.

"Come back home, Lisa," he begged. "I'm not having an affair and I have no desire to have an affair. It's you I want. You're the one I love."

She remained silent.

"Babe, you have to trust me. I just think toward the end you were getting too paranoid."

Her confusion cleared and her intuition kicked in. He was lying, again. He wanted her to come back because of what she would be worth when the lawsuit was over. He was still denying what she knew to be the truth. The fact that he'd cheated on her.

On the other hand, she was feeling lost. She needed to find a safe place to live and wasn't able to afford anything remotely safe. She was afraid Zoe would go off the deep end and hurt her or herself. She didn't trust the woman. Then she realized it only took her two weeks to recognize that Zoe was not a trustworthy person. It had taken her three years with Brian. She was making progress!

"Let me think about it, Brian."

Chapter Fourteen

She returned to the apartment and was relieved to find Zoe gone. She decided to take advantage of the alone time and pray to God. It had been a long time since she'd asked for his guidance. In fact, she was still angry with him for the wreck that ruined her life. However, he was the only one right now she could turn to.

God, why have you left me alone? Why won't you spare me from any more pain? I can't feel your presence any more. I am alone. I feel that you're the only one who can help me, but I don't feel you in my life anymore. My mother always had faith in you; if not for her, I wouldn't even believe in you. God, if you can hear me, please give me a sign that I'm on the right path. I'm weak right now, and on shaky ground. I need your guidance and your strength. Please help me. Show me a sign of where I go from here.

When she was done praying, she still felt as though she was sitting alone in the middle of the dark ocean with no one to lean on. Nothing was different.

The next morning when she got up, she fixed herself some coffee and started looking through the classified ads. She had looked through the entire section and was about to give up, when a small ad at the bottom of the page caught her eye.

Basement apartment, situated in beautiful wooded section by lake. Furnished. Utilities included. 2250 Old Lake Road, Roswell.

She picked up the newspaper and headed out the door to catch the next bus. While walking through town to the bus stop, she paused to admire a beautiful dress hanging in the window of a boutique. One day, she would wear such a dress again. But not yet.

"Lisa!" a familiar voice called out to her.

She turned and came face-to-face with Stacey from Bertonelli East.

Her former secretary seemed genuinely glad to see her. "Oh my goodness. Just look at you! It's so good to see you!"

"How are you, Stacey," Lisa asked a bit self-conscious about her looks.

"I'm fine. Everyone at Bertonelli's still thinks about you from time to time. You should stop in to see us some…"

Stacey stopped herself.

"What's the matter, Stacey?" Lisa asked, wondering why she stopped mid sentence.

"I'm sorry," Stacey replied. "I wasn't thinking. I guess it would be uncomfortable for you to be around Vanessa."

"Because she got my job?" Lisa asked.

"No, because of her and Bri—" Stacey lowered her head.

Lisa thought she would faint right then and there. Vanessa and Brian? Brian cheated on her with Vanessa? She was livid!

Stacey didn't know what to say. "Lisa, I'm sorry, I thought you knew."

"I knew my husband was cheating," she admitted painfully. "I just didn't know it was with Vanessa." But a lot of things made sense to her now. "I have to go, Stacey. It was nice seeing you."

Lisa turned and headed for the bus stop. She was numb again. It was like the last few weeks of healing mentally, emotionally, and physically hadn't even occurred. Would she have to start all over again?

When the bus reached Old Lake Road she got off. She had to walk quite a distance to the house but wasn't discouraged. The walk was invigorating and helped her remain focused on what she needed to do. When she reached the door, she rang the doorbell and was greeted by a woman who appeared to be in her forties. She had very kind eyes and a warm motherly smile. She invited Lisa inside.

"My name's Maggie Frye and you are?"

"Lisa Caulder." She immediately liked the woman.

Maggie gave her a tour of the cozy living room. She immediately fell in love with the painting hanging over the fireplace. The artist had used various colors and techniques and every color imaginable seemed to play out on the canvas. Lisa was familiar with art; it had been one of her passions when she was growing up. In fact, she was going to be an art major until the position at the Sheraton opened new doors for her. She wondered where she might be right now if she had stayed in college.

She inventoried her surroundings and felt very at home. The scene outside the back French doors was breathtaking. Tall hardwood trees surrounded a crystal lake. Several benches were situated around the perimeter of the lake and looked very inviting. She felt oddly at home.

Maggie followed Lisa's gaze to the lake and smiled. "It's beautiful, isn't it?"

"Very."

"Can I get you something to drink, Lisa? Iced tea, a soft drink or lemonade?"

"No, thank you."

"Let's move to the living room and we can talk about the apartment."

The two got situated on a large, comfortable country sofa.

"What kind of work do you do, Lisa?"

Lisa shifted uncomfortably. Would Maggie consider renting the apartment to someone out of work? "I used to be in catering for a hotel. I booked banquets and food functions."

"That sounds exciting," Maggie said.

Lisa looked down. "It was. And I loved my job. But after the car crash—"

"Oh, dear," Maggie soothed. "You were in an accident?"

"Well, it wasn't really an accident," Lisa explained. "I was hit by a drunk driver. I nearly died."

Maggie reached out and touched Lisa's hand. "I'm so sorry."

"I've been trying to pull my life together for the past year." Lisa suddenly felt self-conscious over her appearance. "My face was completely shattered and I've had more surgeries than I care to recall."

"It must have been so difficult for you." Maggie spied Lisa's wedding rings. She wondered why the young girl was looking for a place to live if she was married. Well, she figured she would tell her when she was ready. Maggie's heart went out to Lisa.

"It has been very challenging," Lisa said with a faint smile. "I don't have a job yet, but I'm looking for one. I volunteer at the soup kitchen over on Fifth Street most days, when I don't have a doctor's appointment or a physical therapy appointment."

"Well," Maggie said and smiled, lifting the mood in the room immediately. Lisa was just the type of person she and her husband were looking to rent the apartment to. "Would you like to see the apartment?"

"Oh, I'd love to!"

Maggie led her down the steps to a cozy little apartment that also had a private entrance off the driveway. The room, tastefully decorated, was filled with light from the French doors that led to the patio. There was a gas grill and wooden bench on the patio and she immediately saw herself spending a lot of time on that bench.

The kitchen was quaint and just the right size for one person. The bedroom was pristine and had a lot of natural light shining through to brighten it.

They returned to the main floor and resumed their seat on the sofa.

"So, what do you think, Lisa?" Maggie asked.

"It's beautiful," she honestly replied. She only hoped she could afford it. She hesitantly asked, "What is the rent?"

Maggie knew that Lisa liked the apartment and wanted to move in. She also sensed the young girl was afraid she might not be able to afford it. Maggie would much rather have a boarder who appreciated the serenity and beauty that filled her home rather than someone who just wanted a place to live.

"Well, how much can you afford?" Maggie asked.

"I worked out a budget and I think I can manage three hundred and fifty dollars a month."

"Amazing!" Maggie smiled. "That's just what we're asking."

Lisa smiled and leaned over and hugged Maggie. "I'll take it!"

Maggie hugged the young girl and gave her a pat on the back. "Then it's all set, you'll move in right away."

"Thank you, God." Lisa whispered. He had heard her prayer and for the first time in a while, she knew he was there. He hadn't abandoned her.

Lisa returned to Zoe's apartment and began packing her clothes. When Zoe walked in and saw her, she became agitated.

"What do you think you're doing?" Zoe demanded, hands on her hips.

"Zoe, I appreciate all that you've done for me, but I don't feel comfortable staying here. I found another place to live."

"You can't do that!"

"I'm sorry if you're disappointed, Zoe, but I think it's best if I leave tonight."

"If you leave without giving me proper notice, you're NOT getting your security deposit back!"

Lisa closed her suitcase and easily lifted it. She grabbed her purse and looped her arm through the strap and opened the door. "Keep it. You can have my share of what's in the fridge, too. Goodbye, Zoe." She turned and walked away. As she continued down the hall, she heard Zoe yelling from the doorway. The further she walked, the more distant Zoe's voice became…and the stronger she felt. In less than a month's time, she'd had the courage to walk out on not just one, but *two* people who were not good for her.

Lisa was putting away some groceries in her new apartment when a knock came at the door. It was Maggie and an older, gray-headed man.

"Lisa, I want you to meet my husband, Jake."

"It's nice to meet you, Mr. Frye." She smiled and shook his hand.

Jake had a hearty grip. "Mr. Frye is my daddy," he quipped. "You can call me Jake."

"Are you settled in yet?" Maggie asked.

"Just about. I'm just putting some groceries away."

"We'd like to invite you to have dinner with us this evening," Maggie said and added, "that is, if you're not busy."

Lisa smiled. "I'd love to. Just give me a few more minutes and I'll be right up."

"Good."

Lisa quickly put the rest of the groceries away and just as she was about to leave, the phone rang. It was Brian.

"I got your message that you found a new place," he said with an edge of agitation. "I thought you said you were going to move back in here."

"I said I would think about it," she replied. "Look, I've got to go. I'll call you later."

"All right," Brian replied. "I love you."

Lisa didn't respond. Instead, she hung up the phone and left. When she reached Maggie's kitchen, she found the woman and her husband seated around a small table laden with plenty of food. She took her seat at the table and it was then she spied two different serving plates with ham; one had large slices, the other had smaller, cut pieces. She knew Maggie did that for her benefit.

"Thank you, Maggie."

The older woman smiled at her.

Jake reached out and took Maggie's hand and outstretched his other to take Lisa's.

"Jake," Maggie stopped him. "Maybe Lisa doesn't feel comfortable saying grace."

Lisa smiled and took his hand and reached over and took Maggie's. "I have much to be thankful for." It had been years since she gave thanks for a meal. Not only did she feel good giving thanks with the Frye's, she felt accepted by them for who she was. She felt alive inside.

"Lord," Jake's began the prayer. "We want to thank you for bringing us together this day to share in this feast. We are especially thankful you have brought Lisa into our lives."

Lisa's lower lip began to quiver. Her eyes welled with tears.

"We ask you to bless this food that nourishes our body. Amen."

When the prayer was over, Lisa dabbed the corners of her eyes with her napkin before placing it on her lap. At that moment, she felt closer to God than she ever had. She then filled her plate with ham and mashed potatoes. She was truly grateful.

The next day at the group house, Lisa was in a good mood. The evening with Maggie and Jake had really lifted her spirits.

"Tell us what you've learned, Lisa," Amanda directed.

Lisa no longer looked at the floor when speaking. Instead, she held her head high and looked the group members in the eyes as she spoke.

"I am much more than my looks," she began. "I have so much to offer people. I'm smart, considerate, kind, compassionate, and thoughtful, and that's just for starters!" She smiled. "I'm more in touch with myself—who I really am. That was tough at first, but it comes easy now. I've learned so many things from everyone here and my friends at the soup kitchen."

She was now able to tell when people—like Brian—were being dishonest with her. She could see hidden agendas and wasn't afraid to point them out.

"I feel good about myself for the first time since the wreck," she finished.

Jeff spoke to the group. "As you all know, our theme this week is forgiveness. Lisa, have you forgiven the people in your life who have hurt you?"

"No," she replied honestly. "I am still holding on to some resentment."

"Forgiving involves three key elements. First, you acknowledge the hurt. Second, you acknowledge how it made you feel. Third, you release the person who hurt you, without expectation. I know it sounds easier than it is, but once you do these three things, you are free to move on."

"I'm really struggling with what Brian did to me. The cheating…how he stayed in the relationship for the money…all the lies he told. The same with Walter Fowler. He forever changed my life and I don't' know if I will ever be able to forgive him. I know I can never forget."

"You don't have to forget, Lisa," Jeff replied. "Just forgive. And in time, you will."

She nodded, hoping he was correct.

"Remember, forgiveness is for *you*, not the other person. Forgiveness allows *you* to move forward…"

His words trailed off in her mind and she decided that today, she would work on forgiving everyone who'd hurt her.

Chapter Fifteen

The bus ride back to the Frye's house seemed to take longer than usual after her therapy session that day. She hated taking the bus, but it was her only means of transportation for now. Today, the bus was especially crowded, noisy, and the ride was bumpy.

When the bus reached her destination, she exited and started the long walk down the side road to her apartment. When she reached the Frye's, she noticed a strange car parked in the driveway. She was so exhausted from working so hard during her therapy session, she didn't give it much attention. And although she was drained, she felt oddly empowered. It was a new feeling that would take some time to get used to. She hurried inside and took a rejuvenating shower.

Afterwards, feeling refreshed, she stood by the opened French doors. The cool March air was crisp and refreshing. The sun shone down on her face and warmed her. She studied the scenery before her. The azalea buds had sprouted and daffodils were peeking through the dirt. Birds were chirping and some geese were sunning themselves alongside the lake. It was euphoric. She took the opportunity to say her positive affirmations.

"I am a worthy person," she said aloud. "I am loveable. I have many talents to share with others…" The more she said each line, the better she felt. The power of self-talk. Then she remembered what her mother said, as a man thinketh, so is he. Actually, those words came from the Bible and she knew that they were true.

Her stomach growled and she went inside and checked the refrigerator.

"Lisa, you in there?" Maggie wrapped on the door.

"Just us," added Jake.

Lisa hurried to the door and let them in. Jake was wearing a pair of old coveralls and looked like he just crawled out of a swamp. Then she saw why.

He held up a string of fish he'd just caught. "Hope you like fish," he said, smiling.

Lisa laughed. "I love fish!"

"Good," Maggie said. "Because we're gonna' have one big old fish fry at the Frye house!"

Lisa followed them upstairs and she and Maggie sat at the kitchen table to scale the fish while Jake prepared the kettle.

"You scale," Maggie directed her, "and I'll fillet."

At one point, Maggie laughed after examining the first fish Lisa prepared.

"You've never cleaned fish before, have you?" Maggie asked.

Lisa shook her head. "How'd you know?"

"You forgot to scale the other side," Maggie replied, laughing.

After they'd feasted, Jake leaned back in his chair, stuffed. "There's more fish, Lisa. Dig in!"

"I couldn't eat another bite," she replied. "I'm stuffed!"

"You could use a little more weight on you," Jake commented. "Don't worry. Look at what Maggie's cooking has done to me." He patted his stomach. "We'll have you filled out in no time."

Lisa laughed. She had gained ten pounds since leaving the hospital and only needed to gain six more until she would be the same weight as the day she got married. Her thoughts turned to Brian and she fidgeted in her chair and played with the food on her plate for a few minutes. Jake knew something was troubling her.

"You're doing more squirming in that chair than the fish did when they were fighting to get free from my line," Jake announced.

It took her a moment to realize he was talking to her. "Oh, I was just thinking about some things."

It was then she remembered the strange car in the driveway. "Did you get a new car, Jake? I saw the Buick Skylark in the driveway."

"The one out front? Nah, that ain't for me. I picked it up in Savannah the other day. Good, reliable car. Figured I could put it on the lot and find a buyer for it." Jake owned a used car lot and made a good living at it.

"Now, Lisa," Maggie warned. "Don't get him started on cars because you'll never get him to stop talking."

"Now hold on woman," he said. "Lisa here's looking for one."

Uh-oh. She needed a car, but she didn't think she had enough money—especially not enough for a nice Buick Skylark. She only had two thousand dollars left from the money she borrowed from her mother and that needed to last until she found a job.

Jake seemed to read her mind. "Why don't you just test drive it for a while…just until you make up your mind?"

"I don't think I could afford…" her voice trailed off.

Jake smiled. "How do you know if you can afford it or not when I ain't even told you the price yet?"

Lisa smiled, too.

"How much do you have put aside for a car?" Jake asked.

"Jake!" Maggie scolded him. "That's none of our business."

"Now, Maggie, we're trying to conduct a business transaction here at the dinner table," he teased.

Lisa mentally calculated how much money she could put toward a car and still have enough to live on for the next few months.

"I have about eight hundred dollars I can spend on a car."

Jake slapped his hand lightly on the table. "Maggie, did you hear that? I swear this child was reading my mind. That's exactly how much I was going to ask for the car!"

Maggie and Jake exchanged knowing glances before Maggie reached over and took Lisa's hand.

"You need a car, Lisa. You can't keep taking the bus everywhere. It's not safe," Maggie warned. "With the car, you'll be able to leave when you want and not have to wait on the bus…you'll be able to look for a job…and you'll be able to bring home more than one bag of groceries at a time."

Jake handed her the keys. "Take 'em. If you can pay eight hundred now, okay. If not, you pay me when you have the money."

Lisa's eyes glossed over. "I don't know what to say." No one had ever been this kind to her in her life.

"There's nothing to say, Lisa." Both Maggie and Jake rose from their seats to give her a hug.

Chapter Sixteen

Dressed in one of her business suits, Lisa opened the door of her Skylark and tossed her briefcase onto the passenger's seat. She waived to the Frye's who were standing at the door to see her off. Maggie had made her homemade pumpkin bread for breakfast that morning and Jake brewed her a cup of coffee. They were almost as excited as she was about searching for a job.

She reached over and opened her briefcase. She wanted to take one more look at her resume. It was fine. Maggie read over it several times the night before and assured her it was perfect. They believed in her and that helped her believe in herself. Still, butterflies filled her stomach. She took a couple of deep breaths. She was ready to soar!

She pulled into the parking lot of the first hotel on her list. She was nervous about her appearance—her face, specifically. But that was from residual feelings of inadequacy. As she entered the hotel lobby, she continued to repeat her positive affirmations. "I am a beautiful person inside and out; I have many gifts to offer; I am successful…" she said to herself.

She entered the elevator and pushed the button to the floor where the executive offices were located. Once there, she was directed to take a seat and someone would be with her shortly. She nervously tapped her foot while she waited and finally a man exited an office and introduced himself to her. Although he wasn't rude to her, he certainly didn't appear friendly. He invited her into his office and she handed him her resume before she took her seat. He scanned over it and looked up at her.

"Well," he began. "You're resume is impressive, but we're actually looking for someone who's a little more, uh, outgoing. Someone a little more aggressive. You understand." He handed her resume back to her and thanked her for coming.

Yes, she understood perfectly. How did he know she wasn't aggressive? How did he know she wasn't outgoing? What he really meant to say was he was looking for someone more *attractive.*

All in all, she'd visited eleven hotels that day and was greeted with more of the same. No one even asked to keep her resume. It was as though they took one look at her face and without even considering her credentials or track record, they decided she wouldn't do. Feeling defeated, she returned to her apartment.

Once inside, she threw her briefcase on the sofa and kicked off her shoes. After changing into casual clothes, she headed for the porch swing. There, she gently rocked back and forth and reflected on her day, and what she could have done differently. Nothing...

She watched the trees swaying in the breeze and was lulled into a relaxed state. The view before her was breathtaking. She wondered why the same God that created this beauty could take hers away. But it was only a fleeting thought and at least she hadn't finished the thought with *It isn't fair!* She no longer dwelled on what was fair and what wasn't. Instead, she concentrated on moving forward.

"Ah, there you are," Maggie greeted her. "Can I join you?"

"Yes." Lisa moved from the center of the porch swing to the side.

Maggie took a seat beside her. She knew Lisa well enough to know she didn't have any success that day. The swing gently glided back and forth with neither woman speaking. A flock of geese flew overhead and broke the silence.

"Rough day, huh?" Maggie asked.

Lisa nodded. "Eleven hotels and twelve rejections."

"How could you get twelve rejections from only eleven hotels?"

"I tried to use one of my credit cards to buy lunch. It was denied," she explained. "Brian must have closed the account."

They continued swinging in silence until Maggie spoke up.

"This is just a hiccup," she said. "You know that don't you?"

"I know. But sometimes I get caught up in the way 'they' think. I mean, I used to be pretty and I usually got everything I wanted because of that. Today, all anyone could see about me was my face. Not my qualifications. Not my intelligence. Just my face. And they based their decision on my looks only. I wasn't attractive enough."

"I wish I could say I know how you feel," Maggie stated, "but I don't. I've never been pretty so I don't know how it feels to lose something like that. I've always just been me."

"I think you're beautiful, Maggie," Lisa said truthfully. She now knew what real beauty was. "If I could go back in time, I would change so many of my actions. I mean, I used to judge people on their looks. If they weren't attractive, I didn't have time for them. Now I'm being judged the same cruel way I judged others."

She turned to Maggie and continued. "When I lived in Washington, my friend Sandra and I would go out dancing. If a guy came up to me and asked me to dance, and he wasn't gorgeous, I wouldn't dance with him! I can't believe I was that shallow. I'm so ashamed of my behavior."

Maggie didn't say anything. She knew it was sometimes better to just listen. She kept the swing swaying back and forth while Lisa continued processing. The sun dipped below the horizon and the clouds took on a pink and purple hue. Lisa leaned her head back, closed her eyes, and listened to the crickets.

"Sometimes I wish I had stayed in college and continued with my art studies," Lisa said. "I really love art and thought I would have a career in it but now I don't know what I am supposed to do."

" Maybe the hotels turned you down because you're not supposed to be in that business. When God closes one door he always opens another. Have you prayed about it?"

"Yes, I have. I felt so far away from God right after my car crash but now I feel his presence once again. I believe he brought me here to your house." Lisa replied.

"They say God works in mysterious ways, well I think he is going to really use you to help others from your experience."

"I think so too," Maggie. I don't know what that is right now, but I'm sure he will let me know when the time is right."

Maggie smiled and nodded. "Did I tell you my son is moving back to town in a few weeks? He accepted a new job as an art therapist."

"No, you didn't. What's an art therapist?" she asked.

Maggie laughed. "I'm not quite sure, but I know my son's excited about the position."

Lisa thought for a moment. "I would like to meet him and find out more about art therapy."

"He always comes over for dinner when he's in town. We'll make it a special evening. I think the two of you will get along fine."

It would be nice to meet someone who might be able to reconnect her with her love of art.

"C'mon," Maggie said. "I've got chicken in the oven and you can help Jake and me eat it."

The elevator came to a sudden stop at the eighteenth floor. Lisa patiently waited for the doors to open and exited when they did. She glanced at the directory, found the office number for Annette Felder, and headed down the hall.

Once inside the plush office, she checked in with the secretary and took a seat. An issue of Vogue magazine caught her attention and she leafed through the pages. After fifteen minutes of viewing the beautiful women on the pages, she tossed the magazine aside. She'd rather count the ceiling tiles.

"Mrs. Felder will see you now," the secretary announced and ushered Lisa into the woman's office.

Annette Felder shook Lisa's hand and directed her to take a seat.

"It's nice to meet you, Mrs. Fel—"

"Now then," the attorney spoke. "Let's get down to business."

Oh no, Lisa thought. This woman was Emmit Hickson all over again. Red flags immediately went off.

"I read the journal you dropped off last week and you have a strong case. I think we can take him to the cleaners."

"I don't want to take him to the cleaners," Lisa corrected. "I just want a divorce."

"Right," the woman nodded. "Now, let's talk about my fee."

"Well, I—"

"Mr. Hickson tells me you're still waiting on the appeal from Kinderland Auto Sales. Is that correct?"

"Yes, but—"

"I've worked with Mr. Hickson and my money's on him."

Lisa was agitated and shifted in her chair. This attorney's only interest seemed to be a cut of her settlement. No wonder Emmit Hickson referred Lisa to her. She was just like him! It was all about the money.

"So what I'll do," the attorney prattled on, "is promptly arrange separate maintenance from—" she shuffled some papers around on her desk. "What's his name?"

Lisa frowned. "Brian. Brian Caulder."

She snapped her fingers. "That's right. Then, you can pay me when you get your settlement. And if that shyster Hickson believes you're going to win your suit, your credit's good with me."

Lisa left the attorney's office feeling apprehensive. She soothed her anxiety by telling herself she didn't have to like her divorce attorney. She remembered Stuart's lawyer joke and smiled to herself.

After weeks of looking for a position with no luck, Lisa finally took a job at Elrod's Sandwich Shop. Elrod's was located on the main floor of one of Atlanta's high-rises. Elrod Pertle, the owner, was hard at work trying to keep up with the flow of patrons during the busy lunch hour.

"Let's go, Lisa!" he called to the newest employee. "These sandwiches ain't gonna make themselves."

"Don't pay him any attention, honey," one of the older ladies working in the kitchen said. "He's like that with everyone."

He's a jerk, Lisa thought.

"I said pick it up, Lisa! We got people who need to get back to their office before the hour's up. If they're late, they won't eat here anymore!"

Lisa grabbed a paper towel and wiped the sweat from her forehead. She was about to wash her hands when Elrod continued his badgering.

"What the hell are you doing?"

"I'm wiping my forehead!" Lisa shouted back, tired of his ranting. No human being deserved to be treated like this. "What does it look like I'm doing?"

"It looks like you're primping...and I ain't paying you to primp. Now let's go! I've had it with your slowpoke attitude and forgetting your orders. You got brain problems or something? If it wasn't for that sweet little ass of yours, I wouldn't keep you around."

That was the final straw. She turned away from the sandwich she'd been preparing and walked over to him.

"The only problem I have, Mr. Pertle, is with you and the way you treat your employees. So take your silly little hat," she said as she removed it from her head and placed it on his balding head, "and your silly apron," she let it drop to the floor, "and..."

She stopped before she said something she would regret but he got the point. His eyes bulged in disbelief while those who'd witnessed what she did fought to keep from laughing or smiling for fear that they'd get into trouble.

With that, she retrieved her purse and waltzed out the door.

Lisa's mood was just as bleak as the weather outside. She sat on a chair inside the French doors and watched the rain cascade down the glass pane. The steady rhythm of the drops hitting the wooden deck lulled her into a relaxed state. At least she wasn't feeling anxious any more over the day's events. She didn't even regret what she did to Elrod Pertle. He deserved it.

There was a knock at her door and she wondered who it could be. It wasn't Maggie or Jake; they always used the inside door.

She opened the door and was surprised to find Brian standing there, soaking wet.

"Hi, babe. Can I come in?"

Although she didn't feel up to a visit with him, she felt it would have been rude to let him stand in the rain. Reluctantly, she invited him in and fetched a towel.

As he was drying off, he paused to look at her. "I got served with the divorce papers today." He handed her the towel. "Babe, please don't do this. I love you."

She hardened her heart. "Look, Brian, I've had a hard day and I really don't have time to—"

He tried to reel her in. "Babe, what happened? You can talk to me."

"I quit my job today, that's what happened. So I'm really not in the mood—"

"Lisa, don't worry. I can take care of you," he said, trying to take advantage of her vulnerability. "Get your things and I'll take you home. We can call off the divorce and start over. We're good together, babe."

Lisa looked into his eyes while he spoke and she saw nothing but emptiness in them. It was like he had no soul.

"We were only good together when I was who you wanted me to be, Brian," she said and quickly added, "Oh, and when I had a pretty face."

"How can you even say that, Lisa?" he continued. "I can't live without you."

She looked him straight in the eye. "Well, I *can* live without you and that's what I intend to do."

Brian was becoming agitated at her resistance. He'd always been able to smooth talk her in the past and was frustrated that she wasn't buying into it now. "How can you say that?"

"Ask Vanessa," she said without feeling. "By the way, how is Vanessa?"

Damn! He wondered how she found out. "Look, I won't lie to you. Vanessa and I were together, but that's over now. She didn't mean anything to me. I love you. I have always loved you. You're all I want. All I want to do is take care of you."

She moved to the door and opened it. "And all I want to do is move on with my life."

He could tell she wasn't going to budge. The one thing he thought he could always rely on—her dependence on him— was finally gone. He had lost control of her *and her settlement.*

"Please leave," she directed.

"All right. I'll go. But promise me that you'll think about dropping the divorce."

"You just don't get it, Brian," she shook her head.

His anger kicked in and as he walked outside, he turned and warned. "You'll be sorry if you don't take me back."

She slammed the door and leaned into it. She felt sorry for Brian.

Later that evening, she sat in Maggie's living room in front of the fireplace drinking a cup of coffee with the older woman.

"I wish I could have seen Elrod's face when you did that," Maggie laughed.

"I've never done anything like that, Maggie. You should have seen me, I was shaking."

"Yea, but you didn't let it show. You stood up to that jerk. It was about time someone did. Maybe his other employees will have it easier after what you did."

Lisa hadn't thought of that before. She hoped Maggie was right.

"Brian came over this evening."

"We saw his car," Maggie said. "We don't want you to think we're spying on you, we just want to make sure you're okay."

Lisa reached out to touch Maggie's hand. "Thank you. I know you're not spying and I'm glad you watch over me at times."

"So what did he have to say this time?"

"He got served the divorce papers today. He wants me to drop the filing and move back in with him."

"Hah!" Maggie quipped. "He doesn't deserve someone like you." The older woman looked at her. "What'd you tell him?"

Lisa smiled. "I told him to leave."

"Good for you!" She stoked the fireplace. "I can't wait for you to meet our son, Kevin."

Lisa cocked her head. "Maggie, you're not trying to set me up with your son, are you?"

"Oh, good heavens. What a thing to ask," Maggie tried to cover her tracks. "Goodness, you're making such progress on your own. The last thing you need is a man in your life."

"You've got some empty space on the mantle," Lisa replied, smiling. "You could put the Oscar there." She knew all too well that Maggie was indeed fixing to set her up with her son. She didn't care. She loved the older woman and knew she had her best interest at heart.

Chapter Seventeen

The phone startled Lisa from her slumber early the following morning. She groped for the phone on the nightstand.

"Hello," she answered it in a groggy voice.

"Good morning, Lisa. Annette Felder. How are you this morning?"

Lisa sat up and smoothed her hair from her face. Why was her attorney calling at this hour?

"Fine, I guess."

"Good, good. Listen, I'm afraid I have a bit of bad news for you. Your husband is going for a jury trial in the divorce."

"What does that mean?"

"It means that he would prefer twelve people hear his side of the story rather than a single judge."

"How will that affect the divorce?"

"Well, a jury trial will take a lot longer and obviously cost you more money. According to Brian's attorney, he doesn't want the divorce; he wants to stay married."

"What he wants is to buy more time so that we're still married when my lawsuit is settled. In the meantime, I am barely making it on the small amount of alimony I get now. I just applied for food stamps. By the way, I thought you were working on getting me an increase."

Lisa was audibly frustrated with her attorney. It seemed the woman wasn't really assisting her. It almost felt like she, too, was hanging around until Lisa's lawsuit was settled and the money awarded.

The tone in Annette's voice clearly conveyed she didn't like to be confronted. "I'm working on getting you more money, that's what I've been doing. It does take time you know."

"How much time? Days? Weeks? Months? And tell me, is Brian on food stamps?"

Annette was agitated. "Well, I wouldn't know. Isn't there a friend or relative you could—"

"Is Brian relying on a friend or relative?" Lisa shot back.

"I'll see what I can do." Click.

Lisa tried to go back to sleep but was too furious. She tossed and turned for an hour and finally decided to get up. It was going to be a long day.

After making a cup of coffee, she strolled down to the lake and settled on a large rock on the bank. The sun reflected brightly off the water and the sight soothed her. This was often where she came to talk to God.

"I can't get through this on my own. Give me strength God. I need your help," she prayed aloud. "I don't want to hurt anyone, not even Brian. I just want to be free to move on."

A wave of peacefulness washed over her and she knew that regardless of all her woes, she was right where she was supposed to be.

She thought back to her childhood and her relationship with God then. She always went to church, but it hadn't meant much to her. The only time she prayed while growing up was when she *wanted* something. She never prayed to give thanks for the things she *had*.

Over the past year, she'd asked herself a million times why the drunk driver had to hit her. She never found an answer. Now, she wondered if the crash happened to bring her back to God. She smiled at the revelation—and gave thanks to God for it.

She returned to her apartment and after a second cup of coffee got dressed and headed out the door. It would be another laborious day of job searching. She wasn't sure if she could ever hold down a job like the one she had at Bertonelli's—simply because of her memory problems. But she knew she could never work at a place like Elrod's Sandwich Shop.

Her first stop was a small office that had advertised for a receptionist. She filled out an application and left it with the secretary who took it and gave her a "We'll call you" smile. Lisa smiled back even though she knew she would not hear from the office.

Next stop, ladies clothing store. She had worked in retail while in college and knew she could easily handle a job like that.

Wind chimes played when she opened the door and several women looked in her direction, but no one came to offer assistance, which was unusual in a clothing boutique. She approached one of the women who was wearing a name tag and asked to speak to the manager about the position that was available. The manager brought her an application and she filled it out and returned it to the manager.

"We'll give you a call," she was told in that same tone that really meant "Thanks, but we're actually looking for someone with more eye appeal."

Her last stop was a telemarketing firm. Not exactly a career aspiration, but if she could land the job, it would do for now. Besides, the person hiring wouldn't have to worry about her looks since it was phone work.

She found the building and entered. An older man looked up from his desk and took the chewed cigar from his mouth. "Yea?"

His desk was in complete disarray and seated behind him were three women who turned to look at her. They were all smoking cigarettes; in fact, there was a smoky haze that filled the room. Her eyes stung and began tearing. Although she'd lost her sense of smell, she could tell her body was rejecting the cigarette smoke when her lungs began to close up. She could never work here. It wasn't healthy.

"I'm sorry, I must be in the wrong building."

She left.

Before heading back to her apartment, she decided to stop at the soup kitchen and say hello to her friends. They were pleased to see her, and almost as disappointed as she was that she'd yet to find a job. They laughed when she shared her story about Elrod. As she left, she realized she missed them as much as they missed her.

She curled up in the wicker chair on her patio and looked out over the lake. Would she ever find a job? What was she doing wrong? Was she trying to reenter the world as the old Lisa and it was conflicting with who she was now?

She remembered Peter from her days at the Sheraton in Washington, D.C. She could learn a lesson from him. He had liked her for who she was back then, not who she pretended to be. He'd been wise and she now wished she had given him more of her attention. Whereas she once thought of herself as knowing more about the world than he, she wondered if he knew more about the meaning of life than she *ever* had. He'd even had Brian pegged back then for the superficial, arrogant person he really was. Oh how she wished she'd paid more attention to him.

There was nothing she could do now except learn from that. She now knew that she could learn from everyone—not just the rich, attractive, and worldly.

The phone rang. She jumped up from the chair and went inside to get it.

"Hello."

"Lisa, it's Amanda from group."

"Amanda, how are you?"

"Not good. Listen, I have some bad news to share with you. Is there someone there with you?"

"Maggie and Jake are home," Lisa replied. "Amanda, what's wrong?"

"This is always a hard thing for a therapist to do, and there's no easy way to do it. Charles Stanford, from group, committed suicide this afternoon. I wanted to tell you before you read about it in the newspaper."

"No," she sighed. "Not Charles. He had so much to live for! How could he do that?"

"Sometimes that negative voice just gets too loud, Lisa. He must have felt hopeless."

Lisa softly cried.

Of Face Value

"Lisa, he mentioned you in a note he left."

"Me? Why me?"

"Jeff's here with me, I'll let him share it with you." Amanda handed the phone off to Jeff.

"Lisa, I'm sorry we had to call with bad news."

"I don't understand," she replied. "I thought Charles was getting better. I was sure he was going to be fine once he graduated."

"Let me read part of the note for you, Lisa: *By now, you know what I've done. Please don't be angry. I watched you rise from a scared and confused person into a very confident woman. You need to be out in the world — I don't. When they told me I was about to graduate, I just couldn't handle it. I felt safe in the group house. Lisa...Nice Lisa...I could have loved you so. Goodbye.*"

Jeff heard her sniffle through the phone. "Lisa, how do you feel hearing that?"

"I'm angry, that's how I feel. I will never forgive him for bailing out. How did he do it?"

"Overdosed on barbiturates. He went peacefully," Jeff replied. "Lisa, we're here if you need to come in and talk about this."

"I know," she said. "Thank you."

They said their good-byes and Lisa no sooner hung up the phone, that it rang.

"Lisa, it's Chad," her brother announced.

"Chad, what are you doing calling me? Is mom okay?"

"Relax, Sis," he replied nonchalantly. "I have good news."

Bad news and good news within the blink of an eye.

"I just wanted to call and tell you that I stopped drinking and have been going to AA meetings. I haven't had a drink in six months and I wanted to call and tell you that it's because of you that I stopped."

187
187187187

Lisa closed her eyes and said a prayer of thanks to God.

"Chad, I'm proud of you," she told him. "Is mom there? I just received some bad news and I need to talk to someone."

"Sure. I'll put her on. Love you, Sis."

Lisa's mother came to the phone.

"Lisa, Chad said something's wrong. What happened?"

She told her about Charles committing suicide.

"Mom, you always said everything happens for a reason, but I don't know what the reason for this is. It's senseless."

"God is strengthening you, Lisa. I know it feels like you can't carry anymore, but you will learn and grow from all these trials. You will be a better person for it. Just have faith, Lisa."

After talking to her mom, she felt better and made some chicken soup.

Lisa sat outside the courthouse on a small wooden bench and glanced at her watch for the third time. Annette Felder was half an hour late by the time she finally showed up.

"I didn't think you were going to show up," Lisa said with irritation in her voice.

"I just got a little tied up," Annette placated her client. "I got the paperwork from Brian's attorney and there's been a change."

"Not another delay," Lisa groaned.

"No," the attorney replied. "Brian will agree to the divorce, but you have to relinquish the alimony."

"What?" Lisa replied. "What will I live on? How will I pay my bills? I thought you were trying to get me *more* money to survive until the settlement—not less!"

"Brian's attorney must have directed him."

Lisa thought for a moment. "If I agree, will it get me my divorce?"

"Absolutely."

Lisa was fuming. She knew Brian was only trying to delay the divorce in hopes that they'd still be legally married when her settlement came through. As it was, she needed every penny of the settlement money just to pay her medical bills and legal fees. If she had to split the money with Brian, or give him a portion of it, she'd be right back where she started—in major debt!

Annette was becoming impatient with her client. "I think you should just sign the papers. You're going to end up paying him one way or another. You might as well do it now."

Lisa sighed. "I guess you're right. How long will all this take once I sign the papers?"

Annette clumsily pulled a few papers out of her leather briefcase. "That's the beautiful part. Just sign these papers and I'll present them to the judge."

Something wasn't right. Lisa wasn't sure what, but something didn't feel right. If it had been this easy all along, why had Annette waited so long to present this to Lisa? "What are they?"

"Releases mostly," Annette replied. "This one says you won't prosecute Brian. This one says you relinquish any and all alimony. And this one says you won't bring any charges against Brian for anything connected with the divorce procedures."

"I'd like to review the papers before I sign them," Lisa said.

Annette was visibly frustrated that her client was not accommodating her. "Look, I'm in a hurry. These papers need to be filed in the court today. If you want your divorce, I would suggest you sign them."

Lisa gave Annette a wary look; however, she took the pen Annette held out to her and signed the papers. She had hoped with her signature, she was signing away all the bad things in her life—even Annette Felder.

In the courtroom a few weeks later, Lisa sat nervously with Annette at her side. She wondered why Brian wasn't in the courtroom. It was just her, Annette and Brian's attorney who sat patiently waiting for the judge to enter.

"All rise."

As the hearing proceeded, there was a lot of legal jargon passing between her attorney, the judge, and Brian's attorney — she didn't understand any of it. After about twenty minutes, the judge shuffled some papers on his desk and addressed the attorneys one last time.

"Are there any further arguments in the case of Caulder versus Caulder?"

Brian's attorney stood before the judge. "No, your Honor. All is acceptable by my client."

The judge turned to Annette and peered over the rims of his wire-framed glasses that sat comfortably on his nose. "Ms. Felder?"

"Nothing further, your Honor," she replied. "My client has read and understands the agreements."

Lisa leaned toward Annette. "Are those the papers I signed earlier?"

"Ssh!" Annette scolded her.

"Very well," replied the Judge. "The court has read all the petitions and agreements and now passes same into finalization. Brian Caulder will no longer be required to pay any alimony to Lisa Caulder." He reached for his gavel. Smack. "Court dismissed."

"Your Honor!" Lisa called out without thinking. "I thought I was getting a divorce today! I thought that's why I had to sign all those papers!" She jumped up out of her seat and approached the bench before she gave thought to her action.

The judge glared at her. "Young lady, this is a court of law! If you have difficulties in understanding the verdict of this court, please consult with your counsel." He stepped down from the podium dismissing her.

"Your Honor, something is terribly wrong!" she tried again to get his attention.

The judge scowled at Annette. "Counselor, did you explain to your client exactly what was to occur in this courtroom today?"

"In every detail, your Honor. But as your Honor knows, there are times when an individual has last minute thoughts and wants to change his or her mind."

The judge nodded understandingly and turned his attention back to Lisa. "Mrs. Caulder, you have had ample time to go over the agreements and you have received counsel on same. The court will not entertain the possibility of further discussion on the subject."

"But sir—"

He entered his chambers and slammed the door.

"You had better shut your mouth unless you want to end up in jail for contempt of court." Annette's words hit her like a blow to the face.

She turned and walked out of the courtroom without saying a word to Annette.

Lisa sat at the base of a tree located along the bank of the lake. The day's events played over and over again in her mind. That morning, she'd awakened happy and hopeful that she would be divorced by this time today. She wasn't divorced. Instead, she was still married to Brian, and had unknowingly signed away her alimony. Annette had been ruthless.

"I get it, God," she whispered under her breath. It had been her own fault that Annette duped her. Lisa's intuition acted up when Annette showed her the papers a few weeks ago, yet she ignored her feelings that something wasn't right.

A twig snapped behind Lisa and she turned to find an older man standing a few feet from her. He had white hair, a bushy mustache and was slightly overweight. In his arms he carried a lawn chair and fishing gear.

"Don't mean to be interruptin' you when you're talkin' to the Almighty," he opened the conversation.

"I didn't know anyone else was out here," she replied, feeling embarrassed.

The old man unfolded his chair, took a seat, and baited his hook. "Don't mind me. I'm here every day round this time to see if the fish are bitin'."

Lisa wondered if maybe she was on private property. Maybe Maggie and Jake didn't own all the land surrounding the lake.

"I apologize if I'm trespassing on your property," she quickly said.

"Ain't my property," he replied. "In fact, it belongs to the one you were talkin' to when I got here."

He rolled a piece of cheese between his fingers and when it was perfectly rounded, she expected him to bait the hook. Instead, he plopped the piece of cheese in his mouth.

"Name's Major," he said.

"I'm Lisa," she replied, wanting to laugh at his peculiarities. He was certainly an odd character; she couldn't wait to tell Maggie about him.

She stood and dusted off her pants. "Well, Major, it was nice to meet you. I have to get going."

"You have a good day," he replied then cast his line into the lake.

Was this man senile, she thought? He just cast his line without any bait on the hook.

"You forgot to bait your hook, Major."

"No, I didn't," he replied.

"Yes, you did," she gently argued. "If you need help, I can bait it for you."

He didn't respond.

"You're not going to catch any fish like that," Lisa pointed out.

"There's a big difference between fishing and catching," he finally said. "I'm not interested in catching, so I just fish. It's good for the soul." He gave her a sideways glance and she didn't miss the twinkle in his eye.

By this time, she was amused. "You mean you just sit here and hold a fishing pole?"

"Yep, that's what I mean."

She resumed her seat on the ground.

"Since you're not in such a big hurry after all," he said, "how about a soft drink?" He opened the cooler and brought out two cans and handed one to her.

Lisa popped the top and took a sip.

They sat silent for a few minutes, taking in the sounds of the crickets and the frogs. Occasionally, the ducks on the opposite end of the lake would quack.

"You know, this is where I come to do my talkin' to God, too," he shared with her.

"You think he hears?" she asked.

"I know he hears."

Lisa looked at Major and although he was peculiar, she couldn't help thinking he was very wise.

"Can I ask you a question, Major?"

"That's what I'm here for."

"Do you ever wonder why He works the way he does?"

"Nope."

"Never?"

He shook his head back and forth indicating "no."

If Major had that much faith, maybe he could answer some of her questions.

"Why do you think God allows bad things to happen to people?"

"I think He allows *things* to happen," he explained. "It's us that labels them as being bad."

She didn't understand his response. Maybe if she explained her situation, he would understand what she meant.

"I used to be very pretty," she started. "I had a high-profile job in a Washington, D.C. hotel. I wined and dined with ambassadors and congressmen. I was welcomed into Washington society and I loved it. I was on top of the world."

She stopped long enough to take a breath.

"I got married and moved here. My husband and I had everything we thought we could ever want—until that Saturday that changed my life.

"I was on my way to work and was hit head on by a drunk driver. That collision changed my life forever.

"At first, I couldn't even look at myself in the mirror. I looked awful. I wasn't pretty any more." She filled him in on the details of her life over the past year.

"Now, I'm getting a divorce, and I wonder if I'll ever be able to hold down another job."

He nodded as though he understood. "I can see why you think that bad things have happened to you."

"What do you mean?"

"The way I see it," he began. "Some folks just need a louder wake-up call than others."

"I still don't understand."

"Did you love your husband when you married him?"

"I don't know," she replied in a quiet tone. "I was in love with the type of life I thought he could provide."

"I see." He scratched his beard. "So it seems you weren't being honest with yourself."

"No, I wasn't," she replied. "I was so superficial, so arrogant before. I based my entire life on outward appearances."

"And now?"

"Now I recognize that beauty, *real beauty*, comes from within," she replied.

"How 'bout those people you serve at the soup kitchen?"

She smiled. "They are the kindest and most compassionate people I've ever met! I mean, they don't have a place to live, they don't know where their next meal is coming from, and some days, they don't even have the opportunity to take a bath. But they still smile and love and care for one another."

"And you think God took something from you? Seems to me he gave you your life back. You should feel blessed. See, most people have superficial values and go through life putting on a façade. They hide themselves behind their masks of beauty, money, and pride mainly because they are very insecure with themselves on the inside. Take away someone's lively hood like their job, spouse, or their money, and you'll see 'em squirmin' like a fish out of water. Most people don't realize they've been living the wrong way until most of their life has passed them by. Then it's too late and they're angry and resentful that they missed their true calling in life."

Everything he was saying made perfect sense to her.

"I always say *If you paid top dollar for it, it ain't worth nothing,*" he told her.

She smiled

"Now, back to your original question about why God allows bad things to happen. Let's review. You weren't living your life honestly for years. You chose a husband who you felt could offer you a world of material goods. A fancy car, nice house. And you based your value on what you looked like. Am I right in those?"

She nodded.

"And now, after your life was turned upside down by that awful car wreck, you recognize that beauty comes from within; and if you can hold something in your hand, chances are it has no real value; and whereas you didn't have the time of day for poor folks you now feed them at the soup kitchen almost every day. Oh, and let's not forget that you talk to God now."

She smiled again.

"The way I see it only good things have happened to you."

Before she knew it, almost two hours had passed. She couldn't believe how enlightened she felt. She thanked Major for his wisdom and started to return to the Frye's house. She turned to ask him if he would be back tomorrow and she was surprised to find he was gone. She looked in all directions and could find no telltale sign of him. How odd, she thought.

She decided to take a different path back to the house and was surprised when she came upon a hidden dock. As the sun set on the horizon, many colors played out on the lake and she experienced a feeling of deja vu. No wonder. The scene before her was the exact scene in the painting above Maggie's fireplace.

Lisa had just entered her apartment when the phone rang. It was Brian.

"Hi, babe," he greeted her.

"Brian, I asked you not to call me."

"Lisa, I've been doing some soul-searching and I really need to talk to you. Can you come over now?"

"I have nothing to say to you, Brian."

"Lisa, I stopped the alimony because that's what my attorney wanted me to do. I didn't want to."

"Since when do you do something you don't want to?" she challenged him.

"Please, Lisa. This is one of the things I want to talk about. Please say you'll come over."

She thought for a moment. Maybe he was going to offer to start the alimony again. Probably not, but she was hopeful. Besides, she still had some of her clothes at the condo that she needed to get.

"I'll stop by at ten tomorrow morning," she replied.

"Thanks, babe. See you then."

Chapter Eighteen

The following morning, Lisa tapped on the door of the condo. It felt strange to be there. It was as though she was walking through the portal to all her vulnerabilities and insecurities again. It was an awful feeling.

"Babe," Brian greeted her. He kissed her on the cheek. "Come in."

She followed him inside.

"Can I get you some tea, babe?"

"I didn't come to socialize, Brian. I came to ask you some questions, and to get the rest of my clothes."

"Anything, babe. What do you want to know?"

"When will you give me a divorce?"

"I don't want a divorce, Lisa. That's my point."

"Well then you need to find a wife who accepts your infidelity—because I don't."

"I'm done with all that. I want us to really work on our marriage."

She knew his pleading was fueled by the expected payoff— her insurance settlement. Maybe two years ago she wouldn't have seen through his façade, but she did now.

"I want to have a baby, Lisa," he said.

He was certainly pulling out all the stops.

"Remember how you always talked about having a baby? Well, I want us to start a family."

"It's a little late for that," she said. "Look, I'm going to get my clothes and get out of here." How did she ever fall for this stuff when she had been living with him?

"Just think, Lisa. If you move back in, you won't have to worry about finding a job. I'm making a lot of money and can afford to keep you in the lifestyle that you were used to before your car crash." He was sure that would pull her in. "We'll start a family and everything will be great."

She turned and looked him directly in the eye. She was surprised by the compassion she felt for him. He was lost— utterly and completely lost.

She reached out and caressed his cheek. "Brian," she whispered. "There was a time when what you propose would have satisfied me. But not now. The Lisa you fell in love with doesn't exist anymore."

"But you'll be back to your old self soon," he assured her. "Just give it time."

"That's what you don't understand, Brian. I never want to go back to the person I was. I have a new life and I'm happy, really happy, and content with my life."

"I don't understand," he stammered.

"I know you don't. But someday you will." She gave him a kiss on his cheek then ascended the steps to the bedroom to get the rest of her things. While there, a few papers on the nightstand caught her attention—especially when she saw her name. After a closer examination, although she wasn't an attorney, she understood that Brian was filing his own lawsuit against Kinderland in a loss of consortium suit. The more she read, the more she understood the relationship between Hickson and Felder. She also understood why they had maneuvered her the way they had.

She shook her head. They were trying to gain from her suffering.

She gathered her clothes and placed them in her overnight bag. She took one last look around the bedroom before she left. She walked into the master bathroom and stood before the mirror, remembering the first day home from the hospital and how she had been appalled at what she'd seen in the mirror.

Now she looked in the mirror and smiled at the wonderful woman she'd become. She would never go back—ever.

Lisa changed out of her business suit and into a navy blue jogging suit. After running a brush through her hair, she stepped onto the patio to stretch her muscles before taking a vigorous walk down to the lake.

Before she could get a foot off the patio, the phone rang.

"Lisa, Hickson here. I have some bad news."

"What is it Mr. Hickson?"

"We lost the appeal."

She was disappointed, but she imagined she wasn't as disappointed as Brian, Hickson, and Felder.

"Where do we go from here?" she asked.

"Well, the case will be retried unless they make us an offer, which so far they haven't done. But I feel one coming. They don't want a retrial any more than I do. I'll call you if they make an offer."

Lisa said her goodbyes and grabbed her water bottle before leaving for the lake. She hoped Major was there. She had so many revelations to share with him. She visited the spot where he fished and he wasn't there. She looked for any sign that he'd even been there before. Nothing. That was strange.

She found a boulder to sit on and was just getting situated when a dog barked in the distance. She turned and spied a man and dog heading in her direction. She squinted to try to make out the figure. The man was average build so it couldn't be Major.

As he neared, she saw he was younger, probably the same age as her. She was sure the man hadn't spied her; she was somewhat hidden by some overgrown brush. But his dog spotted her, and with tail wagging, took off in her direction.

The man whistled. "Here Boon! Come on, boy!"

The dog obeyed and returned to its owner. The man sailed a Frisbee through the air and the dog took off after it. The Frisbee landed at the base of the boulder.

The dog went for the Frisbee and spied her at the same time. He chose her over the Frisbee and jumped up on the boulder and began covering her in slobbery kisses.

Lisa giggled out loud.

It was then the man noticed his dog was showering the stranger with kisses.

"Boon! Get down, boy!" he called to the dog and rushed over to observe.

"I'm sorry," he said, taking hold of Boon's collar. "I didn't know anyone was here. He didn't scare you, did he?"

"No. He only gave me a well-deserved bath." She laughed.

"I'm Kevin," he announced and extended his hand up to her. She took it.

"I'm Lisa," she replied, bashfully.

"So you're Lisa? I'm Maggie's son."

"Oh! Your mother has told me all about you. It's nice to meet you."

He looked out over the water of the lake and inhaled deeply. "I see you like it here, too."

"Yes. I love it here," she replied. "I was looking for an older gentleman today—"

"You go for older men, then?" he teased.

Lisa smiled, liking him immediately. "Very funny. Actually, there was an elderly man here yesterday I spoke to and I wanted to see if he was here today. I had some good news to share with him."

"Since he's not here, will I do?" Kevin asked, smiling.

Lisa smiled shyly back at him. "I should probably be getting back. It was nice to meet you." When she started to climb off the bolder, he extended his hand to help her down.

"It was nice meeting you, too," he replied.

"Good-bye," she said and headed back to the apartment.

"Would you like to get together sometime?" he called out to her, holding on to Boon who had tried to follow at her heels.

She smiled and called over her shoulder, "That would be nice."

Chapter Nineteen

Lisa nervously tapped her foot while seated in the waiting area of the law offices of Huntington, Paisley, and Davis. The secretary offered her a cup of coffee which she politely declined. She was already nervous; she'd had so many bad experiences with attorneys that she was wondering if this one would have any of the same characteristics as Hickson and Felder.

A tall gentleman entered the waiting area. "Lisa?" he asked, addressing her.

"Yes." She stood and shook his hand.

"I'm Stephen Huntington. It's good to finally meet you in person. Amanda at the Northridge day treatment program told me all about you."

He led her into a large conference room and pulled out a chair for her to sit down.

"Lisa, I don't usually meet with people on such short notice, but your story was really moving. I'd like to help you as much as I can."

"Thank you. I appreciate that."

She shared with him the past year of her life, making sure to include all details—even Brian's infidelity. He only interrupted occasionally when he needed more information vital to her case.

When she'd mentioned Annette Felder and Emmit Hickson, he'd flinched. He felt genuinely saddened that the woman before him got mixed up with those two.

"As of now, I'm still married and collecting no alimony. Meanwhile, my husband, Annette Felder, and Emmit Hickson are all waiting on my settlement money."

"Is your personal injury case going to be retried?"

"I don't know. Mr. Hickson said they will probably make us an offer."

"I'm sorry that you've had to go through all this, Mrs. Caulder," he told her. "I'll take your divorce case pro bono."

"Pro bono?" she repeated, unsure what he meant.

He smiled. "No charge."

"Thank you so much, Mr. Huntington. You don't know what this means to me."

The following morning, Lisa awoke to the sound of the phone.

"Hello."

"Lisa, Emmit Hickson. Can you come over to my office right away?"

"Why?"

"The insurance company made us an offer."

"I'll be right there."

Within a short amount of time, Lisa was seated in Hickson's office with Brian. She wasn't surprised to see him there.

"Hello," she greeted.

He ignored her.

"Let me read the terms of the settlement to you."

She shook her head. She didn't trust him. "I'd like to review the papers please." She held out her hand and he reluctantly handed them over.

After carefully reviewing them, although the sum was much lower than the jury awarded her, she signed on the dotted line. She wanted to have this over with today, not wait another year for a new trial. It had already been a year since her jury trial.

"Great," Hickson said. "I'll deposit the check in escrow and will get the money to you in eight to ten days. I'll take out my forty percent, plus expenses."

She did the math in her head. Hickson got his forty percent, followed by the hospital and doctors. She would get a meager amount; even so, it would be enough to allow her to start over and that was what was important to her.

"And Brian," Hickson handed a document to Brian to sign. "This is your settlement for the loss of consortium suit."

Brian smiled and signed the document. "When can I get my money?"

"Eight to ten days."

"Thanks a million, Emmit, for all you've done."

Chapter Twenty

Maggie prepared a celebratory dinner for Lisa that consisted of her famous fried chicken, mashed potatoes, turnip greens, black-eyed peas, and cornbread. A southern feast indeed.

"You invited Kevin?" Lisa's eyes widened. "Look at me! I'm not dressed up. I didn't do my hair."

Maggie took her hands. "Lisa, you look beautiful. Besides, Kevin's not coming to see your clothes or your hair. He's coming because he wanted to see you."

"I'm so nervous," Lisa said.

"Well don't be," Maggie replied. "Now tell me what happened today when you met with Hickson."

Lisa explained the day's events as she helped Maggie set the table. When they were done, Jake came in and announced that Kevin called and was running a little late. He didn't want to hold up dinner and wanted them to start without him.

In a way, Lisa was glad. She was famished and wanted to eat. They sat down at the table and after the blessing, she dug into the mashed potatoes.

"And how about your divorce, Lisa. When will that be final?"

"I'm not sure. Mr. Huntington filed a motion to dismiss the jury trial. He said it shouldn't be much longer since Brian and I both received our settlements."

"That's good news, Lisa."

"It is, isn't it," she replied then changed the subject. "I was down at the lake today looking for Major again but didn't see him. Have you seen him lately?"

Maggie looked puzzled. "Who's Major, dear?"

"The old man who fishes in the lake," she explained then reconsidered. "Actually, he doesn't really fish. He just throws in his line without bait."

Jake straightened in his seat. "Nobody fishes in that lake to my knowledge. We've been living in this house for twenty years and I've never seen anyone around there."

"That's odd. Yesterday, I talked to an old man who said his name was Major. We talked for a couple of hours. I figured he lived nearby."

"Never heard of him," Jake replied.

Lisa turned to Maggie. "Have you ever heard of him?"

Maggie shook her head no.

Lisa was perplexed.

The front door opened and Kevin walked in with a big grin on his face. He greeted his mother and father then turned to Lisa.

"So, we meet again," he said, smiling.

She blushed. "Hello."

He took a seat at the table. "Looks like I'm in time for Mom's famous peach cobbler."

"You just hold your horses, son," Jake directed. "Lisa, grab some of the cobbler before Kevin gets the serving spoon in his hand cause I guarantee there won't be anything left after he digs in."

Everyone laughed.

"So, Lisa, have you found a job yet?" Kevin asked.

"Not yet. I'm still looking."

"Well, I have a lead for you. There's a job coming open with a company called Destination Atlanta. You would answer the telephone and take reservations for hotel packages. There's no pressure and you could do it part time. You would be perfect for this job since you worked in the hotel business."

"That sounds great, Kevin."

He took a business card out of his pocket and handed it to Lisa. "Here's the guy to call. Tell him I referred you."

"Thank you." She smiled.

The rest of the meal was pleasant and she found herself looking at Kevin every chance she got.

As the days went by, Lisa's transformation was nearly complete. She sat by the lake and thought about Maggie and Jake. She would be moving from the apartment soon and into her own place. She would miss the two terribly; they helped in her healing process and she would never forget them.

She watched the ripples trail across the lake. It was here she mourned the death of the old Lisa, and here she embraced the new Lisa. It was here she learned to live in the moment and not worry about tomorrow. It was here she learned how to forgive. And it was here she learned to accept others through accepting herself. She smiled and said a prayer of thanks to God.

When she returned to her apartment, she fixed a cup of coffee and retrieved the number Kevin had given her. She dialed the number to Destination Atlanta and was interviewed over the phone for the position. By the time the conversation ended, she found herself employed! She was thrilled to have a job that would be fun and not too demanding. She hung up the phone and then tossed the classified ads in the trash. She hoped it would be a long time before she ever had to look in that section of the newspaper again.

The phone rang and she immediately knew it would be good news. Everything had been going so well for her, how could it be anything else?

"Lisa, hello. It's Stephen Huntington."

"Hello, Mr. Huntington, how are you?"

"I'm fine," he replied. "How are you?"

"I have my fingers crossed that you're calling with good news."

He laughed. "You can uncross your fingers. I am indeed calling with good news. The judge ruled that since both you and Brian received separate settlements, neither of you are entitled to the other's award. It looks like the divorce will be granted in a couple of days. Can you be at the courthouse at nine o'clock on Wednesday?"

"Yes! I'll be there."

"I'll see you then, Lisa."

"Thank you, Mr. Huntington."

She hung up the phone and shouted, "YES!"

On Wednesday, Lisa arrived at the courthouse wondering how she would feel seeing Brian again. Weeks had gone by since she'd last seen him and he seemed like a faint memory.

She entered the courtroom and was relieved to see her attorney there. She took her seat next to him. His confident smile eased her anxiousness. She allowed her gaze to shift in Brian's direction. He was seated next to his attorney, his shoulders slumped forward and his head down. She felt sadness for him. She had grown so much since they'd met and he was still at the same place. She wondered if he would find his way; she hoped he would.

She'd been so caught up in her musings, she'd missed the judge calling her name. Her attorney gently nudged her and she rose to take her place in the witness box.

The judge acknowledged her and rifled through some papers before saying, "Concerning your divorce, basically, when you sign the decree you are forever thereafter divorced from Brian Caulder. Mr. Caulder will have no claim to any of your settlement, nor will you have any claim to his."

The judge handed her a form and she read the papers carefully and signed them. She returned them to the judge. He looked at Brian's lawyer.

"Any comment from the defendant?"

"No," Brian's attorney replied. Brian was clearly displeased at his attorney's passive response.

"This case is now finalized and dismissed with no further recourse from any party concerned."

Lisa smiled inwardly and looked to Brian. She wanted to wish him well before he left the courthouse, but as soon as the hearing was over, he picked up his briefcase and stomped out of the courtroom. She silently prayed he would be able to work through his feelings and find closure.

She hugged her attorney and thanked him before leaving the courthouse.

When she returned home, she decided to go to the lake and search for Major one more time. When she arrived, instead of

Major, she found Kevin sitting along the bank. The two talked for a long time. She was finally able to open up and talk about everything that had happened over the past few years of her life.

"Wow," he said when she was done. "That's a lot for a person to carry."

"But I wouldn't change anything," she surprised him with her reply. "It made me who I am today and I like who I am."

"So do I," he replied, and smiled, causing her to blush. "You're a very strong woman, Lisa. Many people have suffered less and didn't make it."

She thought of Charles from group. "I know. And I have to share with you that I was almost one of them. After the wreck, I wanted to die. And when I didn't die, I wanted to kill myself."

"But you didn't. You fought and that's an admirable trait, Lisa. No one can ever take that from you."

The two walked around the lake.

"Kevin, when I had two eyes, I was blind. Now I only have sight in one eye and I can see more clearly than ever."

"Lisa, you are beautiful to me—both inside and out. You are the most incredible woman I have ever met."

"Thank you."

"I have been counseling for nine years. All that time I thought I was teaching my clients. But listening to you today, I feel like you are teaching me. You are an inspiration to me."

"Your story would be such an inspiration to others. Have you ever considered sharing it? That may be your real purpose."

She remembered Peter again. He was always talking about purpose.

"Maybe someday I'll write a book," she confided in him.

"I hope I still know you then so I can get an autographed copy."

"I hope so too," she replied. "Another thing I would like to do is to somehow get drunk drivers off the road. I don't want what happened to me to happen to anyone else."

"You could speak and tell your story. Anyone who hears your story wouldn't drink and get behind the wheel and drive."

"I'll have to think about that one. Public speaking is not something I do well."

"There is a group called Mothers Against Drunk Driving that lobbies to get drunk drivers off the road. Maybe you could get involved with them."

"That sounds like something I would like to do. Thanks for the information, Kevin."

Kevin wanted to ask Lisa an important question but didn't know how to bring it up. Finally he just blurted it out.

"Hey, I'm going to a charity ball at the art museum next Saturday night. Would you like to go with me?"

After their talk, Lisa was very comfortable with Kevin. She smiled, "I'd love to." And she knew just what she was going to wear.

Within a week's time, Lisa was moved into her new townhouse. She kept nervously eyeing the clock. Kevin would be there soon. Was she ready for her first date? She moved in front of the mirror again and straightened her red velvet dress before exiting the bedroom and descending the steps.

As she walked down the stairs, she thought back to the Inaugural Ball. She remembered walking down the steps at the hotel and how wonderful she felt. There were many times that she wanted to be that woman again. But not now. She wouldn't trade all that she had learned for anything.

Kevin knocked at the door and when Lisa opened it, he grinned from ear to ear. He looked into her eyes and saw such depth. He was not drawn to her face but to her beautiful spirit that brightened her entire being. Through her journey to reclaim her life, Lisa had discovered that true beauty is on the inside, and she knew she would pass that on to others.